AFTER THE ULTIMATE VIRUS

Sandra J. Darroch

Published by

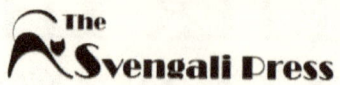

2, 2-4 Notts Ave
Bondi Beach, NSW 2026
AUSTRALIA
sjd@cybersydney.com.au

ISBN 978-0-9946155-3-4 (pbk)
ISBN 978-1-922384-20-1 (ebk)

First published in 2020 by Svengali Press
in association with ETT Imprint

Cover photograph of Bondi Beach by Eugene Tan.

To avoid confusion, the idiom of the late 21st, century has been converted back to that of the early 21st century.

CONTENTS

It was The Best of Times,
it was the worst of times,
it was the age of wisdom
it was the age of foolishness,
it was the epoch of belief
it was the epoch of incredulity
it was the season of Light
it was the season of Darkness
it was the spring of hope
it was the winter of despair
-Charles Dickens *A Tale of Two Cities*

1

THE SPRING OF HOPE

THE LITTLE Colony is perched on a long crescent of pure white sand on the rim of the Pacific Ocean, isolated on a now almost vacant Southern continent. The Colony has been through The Very Worst of Times, surviving The Calamity and the Ultimate Virus. It has been a dire time, but at last things have stabilised. The radiation cloud which still hangs over the Northern Hemisphere is a long way away, and the powerful southerly gales from the Antarctic keep it at bay, which is a godsend for the Colonists. Now, its population is starting to grow, thanks to the Cloning process which has been in full swing.

Colette 850 is one such clone. She was hatched in April 2070 in the Colony Infirmary along with 100 other April clones, and was brought up by her wise old Nanny in the Colony's Creche. Later, as she grew older, she attended the Colony school, housed in the old Public School across the road from the city beach which had once been the world-famous Bondi. After that, she did some private study up to what had been university-level in The Best of Times.

Colette has grown up into a beautiful, healthy, and highly intelligent young woman who works as a Grade 2 operative in the Department of Big Data Verification in the building which had been the Bondi Beach Surf Club back in The Best of Times. Sometimes Colette looks at herself in the mirror and sees both herself-and-her-clone-mother staring back at her: a straight nose, deep blue eyes, long, fine, copper-coloured hair streaked by the sun to a honey tint, a wide mouth, a small mole on her right cheekbone. She has a gentle smile, but there is a hint of mischief or mockery in her expression – and an element of tough determination.

Who was her clone-mother? Did she perish in the Calamity or the Ultimate Virus plague, or had she died before that? Did she have a family? A partner? Where did she live? What did she do for a living? Colette has a burning desire to know the answers to these questions. She doesn't know why – nobody else in the Colony seems to be interested in their clone-mothers, or clone-fathers. Indeed, to look back is frowned upon in the Colony. Things had been so awful, so desperate, and the need for survival so great, that looking backward at what had been is not permitted by the Elders and the Department of Administration, which jointly rule the Colony with an iron grip.

Nevertheless, Colette, who is a determined young woman, vows that she will eventually find out who her clone-mother was. This quest will not only teach her a lot about herself, but is to lead her into a world of intrigue, bravery – and romance.

But before we follow her story, let's take a look at what had happened to the place she has been hatched into.

2

THE WORST OF TIMES

THE BEST of Times had been a glorious series of decades following 2020, the Year of the Coronavirus, or Covid-19 when the planet suffered a collective shock for a while. But recovering from that Virus, the world underwent a period of boundless prosperity, population expansion, scientific triumphs, artistic creativity – and pure sybaritic pleasure. But then came the AI revolution, mass unemployment, endless wars that led to The Calamity and the Ultimate Virus which had snuffed out the last remnants of The Best of Times and wiped out most of the world's population, leaving much of the Earth devoid of a future for many long decades.

But there were some fortunate survivors – 100,000-odd of them, gathered into the little Colony which was founded at the once-famous Bondi Beach, situated about 15 kilometres east of the now-abandoned city of Sydney which had been cordoned-off and left to decay. So far, there has been no sign of any survivors in the other major cities on the southern continent, although a straggle of people remains scattered around the countryside. As for the rest of the world, not a sign of life: No radio signals, no intrepid visitors, have arrived at the Colony. Just dead silence.

That the Colony has survived is due to the way it was established by the Elders. They were practical men and women, experienced in running big organisations, who had weathered the Very Worst of Times and knew how important their task was. At the start, they put the Colony under Army control, commanded by General Walter "Big Wal" Browne, who had brought his troops back safely to Australia from Europe and the Middle East and before nuclear warfare in the Northern Hemisphere broke out in earnest, and the drones took over. Then the Ultimate Virus had hit.

AFTER THE ULTIMATE VIRUS

The Army had done a good job just before the Virus loomed. (They looked back at the Corona Virus – Covid-19 – scourge of 2020 and learned from it.)Teams of soldiers rounded up leading scientists and IT specialists, doctors, engineers, pharmacists, and certain tradesmen, along with a few artists and writers for good measure, and others who would be vital for survival after the Calamity, housing them in a deep underground bunker along with nurses and other useful people, who had work to do, both during and after the Viral plague. This vital group of men and women were administered doses of an experimental drug that was so new it hadn't undergone any trial, even on monkeys – in the desperate hope that it might save them. And, to the delight of the doctors, not to mention the eminent patients themselves, they survived the Ultimate Virus unscathed. This special group did not, however, contain any politicians – as Big Wal observed wryly: "Who wants more trouble? They've done quite enough mischief in the past. A new bunch is bound to emerge later on anyway."

Meanwhile, the Virus was raging through the community and the pharmacists were working around the clock to produce as many doses of the new drug as possible for the local population. Finally, "Big Wal" and his men went out and managed to rescue 90,000-or-so poor wretches from the suburbs, some of whom had already survived the Virus, others were swiftly inoculated – a few of them were parentless young children – all desperate to be rescued from their suburban hell, surrounded as they were by the rotting corpses of their unfortunate relatives and neighbours who had succumbed to the Virus too early. With no hologram-TV to watch, because it had been cut off by the war drones, and with food supplies running out fast, the survivors realised their best bet was to opt for the sanctuary of the Colony, each of them allowed to bring just one precious item from their homes. Some heaved a favourite piece of furniture, some an ancestral family portrait or a precious photograph album or disc, A few brought pet dogs on leads, others carried cats in baskets and birds in cages. One woman clasped her goldfish in a bowl. After that, the Army went further afield, as far as it could penetrate the rest of the coastline of what had been New South Wales, way up north and down south, to pick up a few thousand more struggling survivors. Some farmers and other intrepid souls decided to remain behind in their homesteads and modest shacks, able, they reckoned, to live off the land – as their pioneering forebears had, two or more centuries ago.

Big Wal's wife, the auburn-haired whirlwind, Thomasina, had set up a central kitchen for the Colony and begun a creche and school in the old schoolhouse across the road from the beach for the handful of babies and children who had survived the Plague.

Thomasina Browne had at first billeted all who came to the Colony in temporary accommodation in the vacant luxury hotels and more modest backpacker accommodation that lined the beachfront, before settling them into permanent homes in the thousands of former holiday apartment blocks and small houses behind the beach, and then further up towards the Junction. The once-famous Bondi Beach had been chosen as the site for the Colony partly because of its large number of small apartments. It was a healthy place, too, and not far from the warehouses which contained precious goods which would be of future use to the Colonists.

The Army had remained in control of the Colony until the basics, like water supply, a local sewerage system, a wireless network, and fresh food supplies, could be re-established. Water tanks were salvaged from parts of the now empty, cordoned-off city, and before long a few electric cars were back in use, powered by their rooftop solar panels, at least for short journeys. The colonists were fortunate that much of the most up-to-date technology from The Best of Times had partially survived, and, with the help of the IT experts, some of it began to work again. The old electricity grid had been sabotaged and destroyed during The Worst of Times when law-and-order had broken down completely, but fortunately the street lights had solar panels and most of the buildings had solar panels too on their roofs and windows, supplying sufficient power to keep the Colony well-lit, and warm in the short winters. Re-building the old electricity grid had begun, but it could wait a while until more power was needed to be distributed widely. A primitive mobile-telephone base was also set up, allowing the Colonists to use their mobile phones. The resuscitation of the local TV network was also under way.

Getting some semblance of the full Internet back had been more of a problem. The undersea Internet cables linking the vast southern continent to the rest of the world had been severed by the submarine aquadrones which had also sunk most of the ships containing the interlinked computers which made up the "Cloud", and the satellites had been disrupted and nudged off their courses by wireless jamming and destructive hacking – anyway, there didn't appear to be much, if anything or anyone left overseas to communicate with. At least the Internet, though crippled, still worked, using local databases and stored information. The IT guys did their best to try to contact survivors in the other cities dotted around the south continent, and abroad, but to no avail. If there were survivors, they didn't seem to have access to even wireless technology – or if they did, they were keeping mum. In fact, the IT guys had yet to make contact with anyone else anywhere.

Gradually a semblance of normality was established, and the shell-shocked community started to find its feet. A farm was started in the former Botanic Gardens and the adjacent Domain, and soon healthy crops of wheat and vegetables were growing. A dairy and poultry farm was started in the big Centennial Park where once weekend picnickers had held barbecues under the Moreton Bay fig trees, and smartly-kitted riders had exercised their ponies around the equestrian circuit. As for fuel, the soldiers had been siphoning oil and petrol from tanks around the city, putting it into a central storage depot. But it wouldn't las forever.

It was extremely fortunate that the Army and the first, pioneering, Elders had sensibly placed strong controls on the residents of the budding Colony. Imagine the chaos if 100,000-odd people were let loose on the contents of all the remaining shops and warehouses in the deserted old city and suburbs. It would have been a "kids-in-the-candy store" scenario, and the same free-for-all would have pertained with accommodation, with a virtually endless supply of houses and apartments available in a city which had once housed 7-million.

But the Elders had wisely decided that this cornucopia of goods and housing needed to be rationed out carefully to ensure the steady development of a viable community and infrastructure. A digital inventory was made of the contents of those shops and stores in the city and inner suburbs which were still intact after the vandalism and pillaging during the Calamity. The inventories of the warehouses were already digitally catalogued into databases because they had been accessed for online shopping in The Best of Times. This cataloguing allowed vital supplies to be fairly allocated when needed.

The same careful allocation was made with housing. The city itself, having been cordoned off, was a no-go area except for senior bureaucrats who needed access to data held in filing cabinets and vaults around the town. The Colony was cordoned-off by the Wire. This electrified wire fence was partly to prevent wild tribes of marauding Outlander gangs from wreaking havoc on the precious, tiny, population, and partly to ensure that only housing inside the Wire should be available for settlement because providing each residence with running water and electricity needed to be regulated. The Wire also prevented members of the Colony from going out into the suburbs to pillage. This meant the bureaucrats had control not only of the housing allocation but also the movements of the Colonists, along with ensuring that garbage collection and other services were restricted to manageable areas. This, however, contained the seeds of trouble.

Having completed its task, the Army then handed over the reins to the Department of Administration and its bureaucratic sub-departments. The Chief of Administration was a little like the Governor of the original colony back in the late 1700s and early 1800s. The Chief Administrator had supreme power. but was guided by the Elders.

This was where an ominous trend began which was to have dire consequences. The descendants of the first Elders inherited their parents' power, and property up on the Hill above the Colony, but not their moral backbone. They exploited the privileges they inherited, awarding themselves exclusive access to the luxury goods stored in the warehouses. They chose the best housing up on the Hill and infiltrated the bureaucracy's higher positions with their friends, insidiously imposing their control through bribery and corruption. The omens for the Colony's long-term prospects were not good.

Meanwhile, the biggest immediate problem to be tackled was how to increase the population of the Colony. Many of the females had become infertile from the Virus, and others were too old to produce children. For a long time, the Elders pondered how to solve this problem, until one of them hit on the idea of cloning. The process had been pioneered during The Best of Times after monkeys had been successfully cloned back in 2018. Many of the Elders had grown-up children who were destined to inherit Elder status in time. But more people were needed, so the Elders had toyed with cloning themselves, but then they baulked at the idea of seeing junior replicas of themselves toddling about amongst them. Anyway, many more people were needed if the Colony, and indeed, the human race, were to survive. So the plan to clone was widened and they scoured the now-empty hospitals and bio-banks for samples of tissue that could be used to provide DNA for cloning, and found plenty of samples had been stored because everyone in The Best of Times had wanted the chance to have spare body parts grown, ready for when their existing ones wore out. Fortunately, the tissue had been stored.in a hi-tech version of dry ice which was not affected by the lack of electricity for refrigeration after the Calamity. Moreover, with the advanced medical technology in The Best of Times, all cancer-producing genes and other life-threatening diseases had been removed from the tissue DNA, along with other "bad" genes, including the ones that had caused serious mental conditions, as well as criminal psychopathic behaviour.

It turned out that cloning was a bit trickier than they had envisaged, but finally the Primary Clones were created. However, many of these early Clones were faulty, with dreadful deformities, and had been put outside the boundary of the Colony "for the sake of the human race", as the Department of Communications euphemistically put it.

But by the time Colette 850 is hatched from her incubator, the technique of cloning had been perfected, and Colette, like the rest of her fellow Second-Generation clones, is free of many of the genetic defects which their clone-mothers and clone-fathers had suffered during their lifetimes in the Olden Days and even in The Best of Times.

3

AN OMINOUS SUMMONS

ON TUESDAY morning of October 12, 2093, Colette 850 wakes in her hammock and peers out from her second-floor window at the dark ocean across the road. The sea has heaved and rumbled during the night as a strong southerly wind heaped up the waves. Her chatbot, Sam, greets her: "Wakey, wakey, Colette. It's October 12, 6.am. Maximum temperature 17 degrees, 1 below normal, windy with patches of rain."

Sounds like another normal rainy day. Just like every other rainy day, I guess, she thinks to herself as she takes a quick shower in the cold rainwater from the tank on the roof of her building. *Nothing exciting or interesting is ever going to happen again* she laments as she shampoos her hair. The herbal shampoo made by one of the girls down the corridor makes her sun-blanched hair easy to comb out and dry. She puts on her regulation work uniform – a simple black top and trousers – and goes into her eating nook where the conveyer belt has already passed by, dropping off her breakfast tray from the Colony kitchens into her chute.

She surveys the familiar bright yellow regulation cup and lifts the lid off her plate to check the poached egg and fried tomato sitting on a slice of thinly-buttered toast. Her cup of ersatz coffee is piping hot.

"Mmmm, Sam," Colette says to her chatbot, "You've told the kitchen exactly what I wanted. Thanks."

"Not a problem," Sam replies. "By the way, your tomato came from the new plant nursery in Centennial Park, and your egg came from the hatchery down at the next beach to ours. It's all local, though your toast came today from the flour mill and bakery out West, halfway to the Mountains. They've had a good wheat crop this year. Have a nice day."

9

AFTER THE ULTIMATE VIRUS

Just like every other day, Colette muses. Little does she suspect that this day is to be a turning point in her life.

She knots her now-dry hair into a plait and sets off for work, walking along the curve of the beachfront to her office in the old surf club building. A strong surf is pounding into the deserted yellow-white sand and a lonely gull dips its wing into the wind as it flaps down onto the rocks at the North end of the beach. Summer is just around the corner, but today it is still wintery. Colette's office is just below the Level 1 people who work in the Communications Bureau. If she works hard, she, too, would reach the giddy heights of Level 1, doing exciting work and enjoying some of the extra perks awarded to achievers – but not for another year at least.

She asks her compudule to open up the files she'd worked on yesterday. (Like all the workers in the bureaucracy, Colette has a modern compudule, salvaged from the wreckage of the Calamity and resuscitated by the computer guys.) Her task of sifting through all the vestiges of Big Data salvaged from the city's computers before the final Calamity is starting to irk her. Her training has been thorough, and she has been chosen for the job because she has demonstrated a high intelligence and a thirst for knowledge. Piecing together the fragments of data that had survived the Calamity was a vital task if the human race was ever to get back on its feet – and learn some lessons from the disaster that had engulfed it in the Very Worst of Times. But Colette wants to move on to a new challenge.

My clone-mother was alive and still relatively young in the middle of The Best of Times, she thinks to herself. *I wonder how she coped with the Worst of Times? I really do need to find out more about her!*

Colette then sets aside her normal tasks and begins to pursue this idea, sifting through layers and layers of data for some clue about her clone-mother. She doesn't know her clone-mother's name, nor where she had lived, so she is greatly hampered in her search. She tries entering her own name and the date of her hatching, but that also draws a blank. Indeed, every time she asks her compudule to search for relevant files, the screen goes blank and the compudule tells her there is no information available. After a while, she becomes suspicious. Maybe they don't want her

10

to find out the truth? ("They" are the Central Administration which runs the Colony.).

At lunch in the staff canteen, Colette puts her spoon into her bowl of chicken soup. It is the same old chicken soup she has had every Tuesday for the past two years. There is one variety only.

Back in her office she notices a message icon flashing on her screen. Touching it, her compudule announces that she is to report to the Chief Administrator the following morning at 8am. Stunned, Colette immediately thinks the worst: she must have made a mistake in her work. She would be severely penalised. Her chances of reaching Level 1 would be put back a year.

She has never met the Chief Administrator, Marcus 460, although she has seen him around the building. Everyone holds him in awe. He wields enormous power over the whole beachside Community and further afield too in the other smaller communities dotted along the coastline. He is the head honcho even though he is still only about 30. She conjures up a mental image of him. He has dark, almost black, hair and wears glasses, he is quite tall, and he never smiles. There is an air of powerful determination in the fast way he walks through the office, nodding occasionally to a staff member, but not stopping to chat.

The threat of what could eventuate at her meeting with this ogre next morning hangs over Colette for the rest of her working day. Finally, at 6pm she bids her compudule goodnight and sets off back to her apartment.

Rodney, her boyfriend, pops his head around her door and asks if he could join her for dinner. Relieved to have some convivial companionship to alleviate her concerns, Colette gladly welcomes him into her little apartment.

"I'll ask Sam to get them to deliver two dinners tonight," she tells Rodney. "I ordered chicken. Probably chose that because I'd been researching chicken soup the other day. Would you like chicken too, or sausages? That's the only choice today."

"I'll have the chicken too," Rodney decides, flopping down on the sofa.

"How was your day?" he asks, expecting her usual answer of "Much the same as yesterday."

But then she tells him of her summons to the Chief Administrator the next morning. Rodney looks at her in consternation.

"That doesn't sound too good," he says, his grey eyes flickering.

"That is the understatement of the year!" she exclaims, taking their meals out of the hatch and placing them down, hard, on the table.

"It could well wreck all my plans," she goes on. "I had hoped to reach Level 1 by the time I was 23-and-a-half before I had to get pregnant."

She is referring to the Colony's Pregnancy Program. Cloning had worked well for a couple of decades but this artificial method of producing new humans couldn't go on forever: having two identical people, aged differently, was asking for trouble. An older clone, jealous of a younger one, might commit murder – or was it a form of suicide – clonicide? Or vice versa, a younger clone might get jealous of an older one. Moreover, the genetic pool needed to be widened.

Thus, a new way to increase the population in a regulated fashion had to be formulated and it was decided to de-activate every young woman's contraceptive medication when she reached the age of 23, and start her on an ovulation medication and impregnate her with carefully-selected sperm to produce as many babies – ideally twins, fraternal, not identical – as possible. The age of 23 was chosen because it was deemed that by then a woman was old enough to cope with the emotional stress of having a baby which she was then forced to give up to the care of the Community Nannies. It was very successful in producing healthy babies because the donors of the sperm – existing male clones. – and the recipients, the female clones, were very carefully chosen for characteristics that were compatible and most likely to produce top-quality babies. But it was very stressful for the bereaved mothers.

"Now I'm likely to be penalised for something I've done wrong at work – I can't think what – and my chances of reaching Level 1 before I undergo my pregnancy will be set back by over a year." Colette begins to sob. In the whole two years he had known her, Rodney has never seen Colette cry before. He gets up and holds her close, wiping her tears and brushing her hair out of her eyes.

"Don't worry. Colette, I'll still be here for you after your pregnancy, and then you'll be free for two more years before you have to undergo your second pregnancy. You'll manage to get to Level 1 between the two."

Colette brightens briefly, but then the thought of what she, like all the other young women in the colony, has to go through makes her sombre again. She would have to go to the Infirmary where she would be artificially inseminated with the carefully-selected sperm to produce her twins, who, at birth, would be taken away and brought up in the Nursery by a team of Nannies. She would be permitted, if she wished, to visit her babies once a week.

She knows it is vital to increase the population quickly and efficiently. She also knows it is vital to ensure the future of the human race – there is no alternative – but she isn't looking forward to it. This matter has nagged her for some while, but now an even more immediate threat hangs over her: her appointment next morning with the Chief Administrator.

4

FORBIDDEN TERRITORY

COLETTE DULY arrives on the dot of 8am to report to the Chief Administrator, Marcus 460. She feels worried and a little frightened, unlike her normal confident self. She climbs the stairs to the first floor and is greeted by a receptionist sitting at a large desk outside the door leading into the main department. CCTV cameras beam down on her. She can see a list of sub-departments on the wall behind the receptionist, and a large sign headed"
OUR CHARTER
Under the heading is the Declaration of the Colony, words so familiar to Colette from every Sunday Community Meeting:

- We pledge to save the Human Race
- We obey the Elders & the Chief Administrator
- We do not stray outside the Wire

The receptionist asks her to sit and wait until the Chief Administrator is ready to see her. While she waits, Colette takes in some other notices on the glass door of the department:

Agriculture
Accommodation
Health
Law Enforcement
Technology
Recovered Resources

So this is what Administration people did. What would she be doing when she eventually reached Level 1? Communications, she hopes.

FORBIDDEN TERRITORY

At last, the receptionist speaks. "You may go in now," she says. "The boss's office is at the end of the central aisle. Make sure you knock and wait for him to allow you in."

Colette walks past rows of serious-looking workers, silent except when they give instructions to their compudules. She reaches the end of the long aisle and knocks on the door which simply says: "Chief Administrator".

A deep voice says "Come in" and Colette does so. This is the first time she's ever seen The Chief Administrator close up. The first thing she notices is his eyes behind horn-rimmed spectacles: penetrating hazel-brown eyes with gold flecks, A row of CCTV cameras is lined above his desk. He gestures to her to sit down on the chair in front of his imposing desk. As she does so, she feels the strength of his gaze and she looks down at her hands in confusion. She is surprised that despite his air of distinction he is quite young.

"Well, Colette 850, you must be wondering why I have asked to see you," he begins, frowning and not leaving his eyes from her. She feels intimidated by his brusque manner.

"I guess I must have done something wrong in my work," she almost stutters.

"Yes," he replies, frowning again. "You have indeed done something wrong. You have been attempting to find out who you are cloned from. Aren't you aware that this is totally forbidden?

"We must not delve into our own past.," he goes on, "We must not attempt to find out what our mother- or father-clone was like, what kind of occupation he or she had. No information about our clone-parents must be known. We are all individuals in our own right and we must develop without anything to hamper us."

"But, but..." ventures Colette. "I just wanted to know what she had done for a living and where she had lived."

"That's quite enough!" the Chief Administrator snaps, getting up from his desk and showing her the door. "Just make absolutely sure you never try to find out about your clone-mother again! If you disobey this order you will be stripped of all your concessions and you'll be relegated to menial work somewhere in the outer reaches of the Colony."

Colette, crestfallen, gets up and walks past Marcus 460. As she does so, she can feel, palpably, the strength of the man. She scuttles back down the aisle past the workers, out past the robot-like receptionist and out the front door of the building and into the road leading to her own office. She sits down at her desk, trembling; she's so angry now. *Why can't I find out about my - clone mother? After all, she was the same person as I am, give-or-take a few rogue genes. But we are still one-and-the-same person. I have a right to know.*

She is about to ask her compudule to open up for the day when she notices a beige, unmarked folder on her desk. Where has this come from? Mystified, she opens it.

The folder contains an official-looking document headed PRIVATE AND CONFIDENTIAL She reads on to see a woman's name and date of birth: Sophie Seagrem, b.1982. Sydney.

Puzzled, Colette reads on.

Identifying characteristics:1676 centimeters, copper-blond hair, blue eyes, small mole on top right cheekbone.

Address: 2/2 Pacific Avenue, Bondi Beach.

IQ: 155+

What is this information doing in a folder on her desk? Who put the folder there? Colette reads the document again. "Small mole on right-hand cheekbone." A shiver runs up her spine. It begins to dawn on her that someone has put that folder on her desk because it contained information about her clone-mother! But who would have known she was looking for that very information? No doubt the computer system which had alerted the Chief Administrator must have been accessed by others. *Well,* she decides, *good on whoever it was. I must find out more about Sophie Seagrem. I'll have to be mighty careful and secretive about this, otherwise the Chief Administrator will find out that I've disobeyed him. I could be relegated to kitchen work for the rest of my life. Sophie Seagrem's address must be quite near to where we are. I'll have a look on the map.*

Calling up the map on her compudule she identifies Pacific Avenue quite quickly. It runs along the south end of the beach and Number 2 is the first building in the street.

I'm going to visit that building next Sunday on my day off, she vows. *But that's a no-go area and there's the massive Wire fence at the end of the beach, so I'll have to make some careful plans on how to get there.*

5

BEYOND THE WIRE

ON SUNDAY Colette attends the weekly dawn service down at the beachfront – there are no churches in the Colony; in fact, there is no religion whatsoever, it being regarded as a major cause of the Calamity.

As they did every Sunday, everyone takes the Vow:

- We pledge to save the Human Race
- We obey the Chief Administrator
- We do not stray outside the Wire

After that the fun begins as usual. Sunday is the one day of the week when everyone can let their hair down – or put it up, or cut it off, or dye it. The inhabitants of the Colony are childish in their leisure time. Hairstyles and fashion are one of the very few ways of expressing one's creativity in the Colony, and each Sunday is a veritable fashion parade for both the males and females. That Sunday, some of the girls have dressed up in 1960s-style kinky Swinging London short skirts and leather boots they'd uncovered in the only shop in the Colony: the second-hand op shop. Others had made straw skirts, Hawaiian-style – like the ones they'd seen in the ancient Hawaii Five-O films up the Mall. – No 3-D hologram movies are available – they had all been destroyed in the Calamity, leaving only old archived shows like Hawaii Five-O which were on old-fashioned film or videotape from the Olden Days. It is a simple, somewhat naïve society, this post-apocalyptic world. The Nannies have brought up everyone kindly but strictly, and the young people are straightforward and happy. The television, such as it is, harks back to the mid-20th Century.

`Drugs are unknown and there is virtually no crime – the only criminals are people who have broken the rules of the Elders' Administration, and they are sent outside the Wire, never to be heard of again.

Some of Colette's friends invite her to join them that Sunday morning at the screening of some Buster Keaton and Charlie Chaplin films, but Colette declines, saying she's seen them too many times already. So they set off up the Mall to the cinema, leaving her to wander around, talking to other friends. Rodney comes up and puts his arm over her shoulders.

"Hi there, Col," he greets her. "Have you recovered from your grilling from the Big Boss yet?"

Colette grimaces and laughs. "Yes," she replies. "I guess it was rather traumatic. But I'm OK now. Feel like coming round to my place for dinner and some TV? They're running some fresh old tapes they've just scrounged from a decrepit TV station out in the old suburbs."

Rodney agrees to come at 7pm and then goes off to join his mates in a game of beach volleyball.

It is a typical Sunday and everyone seems relaxed and happy. The surf is rolling in and blowing back spindrift, and there isn't a cloud in the sky. Colette has an early lunch of a hamburger and ice-cream and then she quietly leaves the crowd and wanders, seemingly aimlessly, a surf towel thrown casually over her shoulder, down along the waterline towards the deserted south end of the beach. The tide is right and when she reaches the high Wire fence at the very end of the beach, she slips off her shirt and shorts down to her bikini, takes off her sandals and packs her clothes and towel into her bag, which she heaves over the fence to the sand on the other side. Then, a strong swimmer, she dives into the quite heavy surf and swims out to where the Wire fence ends. Rounding it carefully to avoid electrocution, she catches a wave into the beach on the other side of the fence and paddles into shore. She walks up to her bag, gets out her towel and dries herself, then puts her clothes back on and walks along to the cliff where a rickety wooden staircase leads up from the beach to what had once been a road above.

Climbing the rotten stairs gingerly, she reaches the road and looks up at the long three-storied building where she believes her clone-mother, Sophie Seagrem, had once lived back in the mid-2020s. There is no number on the building, but she reckons it is the right one, No. 2, because she has checked an old map of the area and had noted that the street numbers were even on one side and odd on the other. Number 1 had been a recreational club back in The Best of Times, according to the map, and was a long way down the other side of the street. Looking up at the building in front of her, she notes that it must have formerly been white, but now it is stained by plants that have grown over the glass balcony railings and trailed down over the side of the building to the street below The decades of wind and rain have taken their toll too, but it must have been a glamorous abode when Sophie had lived there.

Colette steps into the wide entrance to what had been a garage, and peers into the darkened area inside. She had thought the building was empty – nobody, except the rogue gangs, lived outside the Colony. But then she hears loud, rough voices. Straining her eyes through the gloom, she can see that the area under the building is full of people, a mixture of men and women, all of them old. The men have straggly long grey-and-white beards and dirty, torn trousers. Some are naked from the waist up, revealing pockmarked skin, others wear ragged shirts. The women's hair is also straggly and unkempt. Most of them are emaciated. Their clothes are just as tattered as the men's. There are no young people anywhere. Some of the huddled group have only one or two teeth. Then she peers closer: some of them, both the men and the women, have awful facial disfigurements. Colette shudders involuntarily. She has never seen people like this before. In fact, she has never seen anything except healthy, full-bodied people – even the older ones. Her eyes now adjusted to the gloom, she observes that some of these pathetic creatures have only one eye, others have lips that are divided into two halves. Others have only one arm, or just three fingers. Some have only flippers for arms. They have been sitting around the embers of a fire they'd made on the floor of the large area at the entrance to the building. At the back of the area, she sees piles of old, filthy blankets. Some men and women are lying together, waking up from what she assumes was some kind of drunken orgy. The whole place stinks.

Colette is aghast and frightened. Maybe she should get away quickly from this terrifying group? She certainly hasn't expected to see anyone, let alone this weird crowd. She had heard that gangs of marauding Outsiders had roamed around the beach town in the Worst of Times, looting the deserted shops for food and clothing. But she had believed the gangs didn't exist anymore. The Wire had been erected ages ago to keep out those marauders; but that was a long time ago.

She is about to turn back, when a tall man with a grey beard flecked with red, staggers out from the gloom.

"What youse want?" he asks. "Youse from the other side of Wire, not one of us 'ere."

Colette is at a loss to know what to say. "I'm Colette 850," she stammers. "I live up the other end of the beach."

"Youse ain't sposed to come down 'ere," says the man. "We never 'ave visters from other end of beach, other side of Wire. Youse better be careful 'ere. Some of us ain't too nice."

Then, to Colette's surprise, the man holds out his hand to her. "Anyways," he says. "Welcome to Pacif'c Ave."

Colette looks at him closely. She sees a glimmer of intelligence in his brown eyes and she takes his hand and shakes it, noting it doesn't have a thumb,

"My clone-mother used to live here," she explains. "and I've come to see where she lived."

"Well," the man says. "My name's Lorf, and I 'ad a number too when I was a small kid. I got cloned in the early days when some of th' clonin' musta gone wrong. Very wrong. When I was 11 they turfed me out 'cause I was faulty and they couldn't 'ave faulties in the Colony 'cos we was tainted."

"So all of you here are faulty clones?" asks Colette. "I never knew the cloning could go wrong."

"Well it sure did, lassie," Lorf replies. "We're the best of the bunch. Yer shoulda seen some of them freaks in the days when we was youngsters. We all look very old, but none of us is really over 50 – but the faulty clonin' and lack of good food made us grow old quick."

"How did you survive outside the Colony?" Colette asks.

"We scrounged round th' empty shops outside th' Wire fer clothes an' blankets an' we found places like this 'ere ta live in, though most of us don't live upstairs. We need to 'ave a fire to 'uddle round in the nighttime and to scare off th' gangs."

BEYOND THE WIRE

"I didn't know the gangs were still around," says Colette, incredulous. "I thought they'd been wiped out a long while ago."

"Nope," says Lorf, coughing and spitting. "Them's pretty old now but they're still around sometimes. 'An I 'ear there's some young 'uns comin' along too. Youse better make sure youse gets back to your safe Colony well before the evenin'. Ain't safe round 'ere after dark."

"I just want to see where my clone-mother lived, that's all," replies Colette. "And I have to get back before the tide changes again."

The old man nods. "Which flat she live in?"

"Number 2," replies Colette.

"I'll show yer if yer likes," he says.

"Thanks," says Colette. "Please lead the way."

Lorf leads her down a corridor and up two flights of stairs, strewn with rotting fishbones.

"You must eat a lot of fish," remarks Colette as she makes her way through the fishbones.

"Yair, we do. There's a lotta fishin' down the rocks," he replies. "An we sometime catch a rabbit or two on the 'eadland. We cut up our fish on the stairs 'cos the tiles make cuttin' easier." They reach the second floor and walk along a walkway to a small flight of steps leading to a door. Colette notes that its handle had been tied up with old rotting rope and rusted wire. Lorf tugs at the tangle and pulls hard. It all falls off in his hands as he pushes the door. It has come off its hinges because they have rusted through.

"Youse'll have t' find somethin' t' tie it up with when youse leaves," Lorf says. "Otherwise people downstairs will try ta get in."

Colette steps into the apartment.

"Thanks, Lorf, you have been very kind and helpful. I'll be OK here now and I'll make sure I find something to tie up the door before I come back down. See you a bit later."

Lorf pats her arm. "Youse take care," he warns as he turns back to the walkway.

Alone in the apartment, Colette looks around. It is covered in dust and cobwebs, but she can make out a tiled floor and big floor-to-ceiling glass doors looking out over the sea. *It must have been a lovely place once,* she thinks. There isn't much furniture in the main room, just a couple of chairs and a small table. In one corner she spies a desk with a very ancient computer on it, and a rusted filing cabinet.

It's amazing anything has been left here, she thinks as she wanders through to the other rooms. There is another large room, opening on to a second balcony, and two bedrooms – the main one on the opposite side of the apartment from the front door – and two bathrooms. Everything is covered in dust and cobwebs. There is a kitchen too, with glass-fronted cupboards still containing bits of crockery. She tries turning on one of the taps. Nothing comes out of it, and she makes out what looks like a dishwasher she'd seen in an old TV film, and a fridge. She tries to open it, but its hinges have rusted and seized up.

I wonder what happened to my clone-mother – to Sophie? she muses. She feels weird, standing there in the very place her clone-mother had stood 70-odd years before.

I wonder if she lived alone. It's quite a big place for one person, about four times any of our apartments in the Colony.

Colette goes out on to the first balcony and looks down to the beach below. *What a beautiful view,* she looks out to the horizon and down to the rolling breakers below. She goes back to the computer and touches it. The keys had seized up with rust long ago, but she manages to open up the old-fashioned CPU and extracts the hard drive.

Maybe I can learn something from this, she thinks, wrapping it in a piece of plastic she found in one of the kitchen drawers. *I'll take it back and get one of the guys in the computer lab to have a look at it. Maybe some data can be rescued.*

She tries opening the filing cabinet drawers, but they are stuck with rust.

I'll see if I can get back here again with a hammer, a spanner and an oil can, she vows. Then she wanders around the apartment again, peering into the main bedroom which is empty except for a built-in wardrobe. She slides its doors open with some difficulty and looks in. Empty except for one simple blue dress, sagging and frayed on a rusted coat hanger; it is exactly her size.

How sad, I wonder what happened to Sophie?

Then she goes back to the kitchen and searches the cupboards and drawers for something to tie the front door up with. She eventually decides the best plan is to tear up an old apron and some old tea towels for a makeshift rope.

Taking one last look around the apartment, she goes out the door, props it back up, and ties the door handle to the catch on the door frame. Then she goes back down the fishy stairs and out through the downstairs area where the grotesque assortment of inhabitants are re-lighting their fire and starting to cook some fish for breakfast, or was it lunch?

Colette can't see Lorf anywhere – he is probably down on the rocks, fishing, or looking for shellfish for dinner, so she scurries past the old men, some of whom are trying to touch her.

Out in the sunlight, she hastens down the stairs to the beach, glad to be out in the open air. Checking the tide, she hurriedly takes off her shirt, shorts and sandals and puts them in her bag and tucks the plastic-wrapped hard drive into it. She throws the bag back over the Wire, then dives into the surf and swims as fast as she can to the end of the Wire, rounds it and swims back to shore on the other, side, safe.

How glad she is to be back in the Colony! She would take the hard drive round to the computer guys that afternoon. Then throwing her towel nonchalantly over her shoulder, she wanders slowly back along the beach to the Sunday crowd, the sound of pop music and the smell of hamburgers wafting down the beach towards her.

6

MARCUS SHOWS HIS HAND

NEXT MORNING Colette wakes up quite early, despite the late night she'd spent with Rodney. They had watched TV and then had sex as usual on the couch, the hammock not being amenable to such frolics. As she showers and dresses in her office uniform, she thinks back over the previous evening. She had been careful not to tell Rodney about her secret visit to Pacific Avenue. Much as she is fond of Rodney, she doesn't feel close enough to him to tell him secrets.

That evening, Colette had found the program they watched -- about industrial strikes during the latter days of The Best of Times – riveting, but Rodney was soon yawning. He simply didn't want to know anything about the Olden Days.

As she opens her hatch for her breakfast tray, Colette hears a beep, and Sam, her chatbot, pipes up: "Morning Colette. I didn't wake you up because I know you had a late night. But I have an urgent message from none other than the Chief Administrator. He demands you report to him the moment you reach your office. It is urgent."

Colette sits down, shocked. The Big Boss must have found out that she'd disobeyed him by going to Pacific Avenue! There must have been a spy camera on the Wire fence, she decides, because nobody was down that far end of the beach.

A tear of anger trickles down her cheek as she gets ready to leave for the office. She is angry enough, but she is even more terrified about the punishment she will receive for transgressing the Chief Administrator. With a heavy heart, she walks over to the Admin building and up the stairs to the executive level. The receptionist spots her immediately and tells her to go in to the Chief's office at once. Colette's feeling of trepidation increases with every step. This time, she is even more aware of all the cameras everywhere, following everybody's movements, including her own.

She takes a seat opposite the Chief, Marcus 460, and looks up at the camera above his desk, then she turns to him. He removes his glasses, revealing his hazel-brown eyes, and gives her that same penetrating look that she'd experienced on her previous session with him.

"Colette 850," he begins, "We know you went to Pacific Avenue yesterday. The camera caught you on the way back because it is angled to spot anyone trying to illegally enter the Colony.

"You are aware, are you not, that you have disobeyed my instructions that you were never to search for your clone-mother's residence and that you would suffer dire consequences were you to be so stupid as to do so?"

Colette trembles.

"But…" she finds herself almost whispering with fear, although she is still defiant. "It's important to me to find out where my clone-mother lived after I'd got her address details. It is just down the end of the beach." She looks up at Marcus 460 to find him staring at her intently.

"And what did you find when you got there?" he asks, to her surprise.

"Well…" she hesitates. "There were a lot of people living on the ground floor – all kinds of old, disfigured, ugly people. They had a fire in the middle of the floor and they wore rags. Some of them had only one eye. Others had no fingers…" she trails off, recalling the horrors she had witnessed.

"Go on," says Marcus 460 firmly.

"Some of them had a dreadful eye disease and others were coughing. They seem to have only fish to eat and they were very thin. I felt sorry for them even though I found them awful. But one of them seemed a decent old fellow. His name is Lorf."

"Did you find out which apartment your clone-mother had lived in?" Marcus 460 asks.

"Yes," Colette nods, "it was on the second floor. Lorf took me up and helped untie the door so I could go in. The place is fearfully dirty. It hasn't been cleaned for 50-odd years, but it must have been a lovely, glamorous place back in The Best of Times."

"That's enough," barks Marcus 460, thumping his desk with his fists. "You have transgressed all the rules of the Colony. You have put yourself in the path of danger. You have disobeyed my orders and you will undergo a series of punishments. The first is that you will serve a full week in the kitchens."

"But I hate cooking, Mr Administrator!" Colette wails, despite herself.

Marcus 460 takes no notice of her pathetic response.

"And now here is a list of future punishments you will undergo. If you do not behave from this moment on, you will lose your job and forfeit all your credits."

Then, leaning over the desk, he hands Colette a sheet of paper.

"This is the list of punishments. Read it quickly and carefully and then give it back to me and I will scan it and place it in your file."

Aghast, Colette picks up the piece of paper and starts reading it.

To her surprise, there is no list. Instead, there is a brief message, handwritten, which says:

I WANT TO COME WITH YOU NEXT TIME YOU GO TO PACIFIC AVENUE. I AM INTERESTED TO SEE IT. PLEASE SEND ME AN UNSIGNED MESSAGE FROM THE COLONY'S COMMUNITY MAIL CENTRE TELLING ME THE DATE AND TIME YOU NEXT PLAN TO GO TO PACIFIC AVENUE. I WILL MEET YOU THERE.
M.

Startled out of her wits, Colette dumbly hands the piece of paper back to Marcus 460.

He takes it, saying "Thank you Colette, that will be all." And with that, he picks up another document from his desk, puts on his glasses and peruses it, taking no further notice of her as she quickly departs.

MARCUS SHOWS HIS HAND

Back in her office, Colette sits, stunned. What is going on? It was all too weird for her to comprehend. *There was the Chief Administrator being ultra-strict about my visit to Pacific Avenue, and then, instead of giving me a list of my punishments, he writes he wants to accompany me next time I go!* All morning she replays in her mind her time in Marcus 460's office. He had been so stern, yet he had passed her a message that was completely the opposite. It slowly begins to dawn on her that perhaps his office is bugged for sound as well as being CCTV'd. Maybe he isn't really so angry with her? Maybe he really does want to see Pacific Avenue for himself. But why?

Unable to do any real work after such an astonishing experience, Colette instead consults the tidal chart and works out what would be the ideal time the following Sunday to plan her next visit to Pacific Avenue. The tides would be best for her swim an hour earlier than yesterday, around 10am. At lunchtime she goes down to the community mail centre and sits down at one of its very primitive old public computers, checks for Marcus's digital-address and keys it in. Then she enters "Next Sunday 10.30am." Finally, she presses "Send" and off the anonymous message goes. Quickly leaving the mail centre, she walks over to the staff canteen, and, spotting Rodney, goes over to sit next to him.

"You look a bit harassed," he remarks.

"Yes, I've had a busy morning," Colette says calmly, putting down her tray of food on the table. "I'm busy delving into the different political regimes they had over the centuries leading up to The Best of Times."

"Hmm," grunts Rodney as he gulps down his lentil soup. "From what I've heard, we're well off not having political parties nowadays."

Colette looks at him keenly. "I disagree," she says. "I think we need government and politics, we can't just do what the Department of Administration tells us to do, all the time."

"Come off it, Colette!" remonstrates Rodney. "Things work pretty well without all that crap."

Colette holds her tongue and finishes her lunch.

"See you this evening, Rodney?" she asks before she leaves.

AFTER THE ULTIMATE VIRUS

"No, Col, today's my weekly night at the gym. See you tomorrow."

Colette is secretly glad. She needs time to get her head around the events of that morning. How would she cope with having the Chief Administrator, that ogre who terrified everyone in the Colony, coming with her to the place where her clone-mother had lived? What would she say to him? What should she call him? Mr. Administrator? Mr. Chief Administrator? Boss? And why is he so interested to see the place?

She gives up trying to make sense of it all and decides to concentrate on her next assignment. First, she needs to delve more deeply into the events that had led to the Worst of Times, the Calamity and the Ultimate Virus. Like everyone in the Colony, she has learned bits and pieces about what had gone wrong – but nothing about The Best of Times. Some of the older Nannies had survived the Calamity and the Virus. They had lost their husbands and children but still had some fond memories of The Best of Times, when living was easy. They would tell stories about it to their young charges. Colette's Nanny had told her a lot about the good things that had happened, and then she had learned more at school about the bad side of The Best of Times: that the world had got out of control...people were no longer in charge of their lives because computers did everything... people were so rich they did no work and just took drugs...and then came the Calamity with its dreadful drone wars...a series of nuclear explosions...radiation all over the Northern Hemisphere...no electricity...no running water...starvation of entire city populations...and finally, the Ultimate Virus.

But what she now needs to do is to see if she could piece together the politics behind it all. The records, as she knows from her years at the Department of Big Data Verification, are faulty in the extreme. Some Data is completely suspect, the product of Fake News. Other information has been lost after the Internet was hacked over and over again. Then the Internet had partly gone down when the undersea cables were sabotaged by the robot submarines. It is going to be a mammoth task to piece together some kind of cohesive history of events.

Colette welcomes the challenge and sets about her task. It will certainly take her mind off her present, puzzling' predicament

MARCUS SHOWS HIS HAND

****

Next day, Colette calls into the computer lab to see whether the techos have managed to access the contents of the hard drive she'd taken from Unit 2, 2 Pacific Avenue. She guesses they'd be able to crack it – even though her clone-mother's computer is so rusted, and it hadn't been the latest technology of the day either – after all, their main job at the Colony is recovering lost data from computers that had got wrecked in the Calamity.

And sure enough, William, the head computer guy, is beaming as he hands her a small gadget. "Your data has been retrieved successfully. Here it is. Stick this into your compudule and you should be able to read it all."

Colette thanks him profusely. She knows she could trust him not to have read the material on the ancient disc – all he was interested in was how the 0's and 1's panned out. She decides it is safest to look at the contents of the device on her portable module back in her flat, so she runs home and puts the disc device in the wardrobe in her bedroom before going back to the office.

Rodney has wanted to come round that evening but she tells him she has a late work assignment she has to finish and she promises she'll be free of it by the following evening.

When she gets home to her apartment after work, she tells her door to lock itself so she won't be disturbed, and she asks Sam to answer any calls and tell whoever it is that she is busy on an assignment. Then she opens the wardrobe, takes out the device, inserts it into her module and searches through its files. To her surprise, she first of all finds a list of articles written by Sophie Seagrem, with dates and foreign cities at the start of each one. *It looks like she must have been some kind of journalist on a newspaper, before newspapers died out completely! But some of the later items look like blogs or they were the text of TV or radio items* Colette thinks, checking through some of the articles' titles:

BIG INCREASE IN CHINA'S POPULATION... TERRORISM IN BANGKOK... GROWING TENSION BETWEEN INDIA AND CHINA... NUCLEAR THREAT IN GOBI DESERT... DRONE ATTACKS ON

AFTER THE ULTIMATE VIRUS

JAPAN… LONDON GUTTED BY DRONE ATTACKS…

Colette is intrigued. Her clone-mother, Sophie, has obviously been a foreign correspondent. Where did she blog from? And she also did TV and Social Media. There weren't any newspapers by the time of the drone attacks on London, so maybe she blogged as well as did other Media stuff.

Then Colette finds a list of text messages Sophie had sent: some were to her editor, others were to friends dotted around the world, telling them she was planning to visit their countries on work assignments and would like to meet up with them. Some others were of riveting interest to Colette. They were to someone called Jim --very personal letters, all signed "Love and kisses and hugs from your loving Sophie." Some of the letters referred to matters back home. Would they invite the Thomas's to dinner when they were next both home? That kind of thing. Obviously Sophie and Jim were a couple. One text mentions their 25th wedding anniversary. Colette is fascinated by that. Marriage was a concept completely unknown to her and the others in the Colony. *What was marriage like?* she wonders. Another text from Jim also interests her. Had Sophie taken delivery of the new kitchen appliances? Sophie had replied:

Yes, yet another load of state-of-the-art appliances was delivered on Tuesday and installed by the robots today. All, as usual, linked to the Internet of Things. All of them sparkling new. This time they're programmed to force us to have at least three cups of coffee a day, and they ring bells if the fridge isn't crammed with all the latest foods. I'm so tired of being forced to obey the demands of these machines! I know the manufacturers have to shove their goods at us to keep up this affluent economy in The Best of Times we live in. The worst part about it is that if you don't comply with their demands to consume, you're issued with

demerit points and you have to pay more for each delivery.

You know, next time, I'm tempted to store the latest gadgets down in our garage. I'll keep my old machines upstairs in the kitchen, turn off the kitchen link to the Internet and plug the new ones into the power and Internet and the sink in the garage, and let them go through their daily routines down there. They can order new coffee and get food supplies delivered by the robots and nobody will know that I will have programmed all the food to go straight down the sink disposal.

So I'd be free to buy the food I like and drink my single cup of coffee-a -day in peace.

Colette is rivetted by these snippets. *The affluence, the waste of precious food!* They give her a rare peep into life in The Best of Times. Fascinated, she reads on, not even noticing her dinner tray has arrived in her hatch.

Then she finds a diary. It started in 2020, when Sophie must have been about 40, and, she checked, it ended in 2033. It gave an almost day-to-day account of Sophie's life and her career as a foreign correspondent. Colette discovers that Jim, too, was a renowned journalist and later was the Sydney chief of an international conglomerate's news service.

From what she reads, Colette can see that Jim waged an endless battle against Fake News. He sent messages to Sophie when she was away, bewailing his uphill struggle against the false gossip and trivial lies that flooded his IN tray, sent by people who purported to be "serious" journalists.

Sometimes Jim also sent Sophie little messages to keep her spirits up when she was holed up in some ruin of a city, in danger of being fired on by robot, or human, troops. He told her stories about life in Pacific Avenue and the antics of the occupants of the other apartments in their block.

AFTER THE ULTIMATE VIRUS

Our resident TV queen has outdone herself with cosmetic surgery this time, he wrote. **I bumped into her in the car park and I simply didn't recognise her – she's had a total face transplant! I hear she's about to star in a new program all about cartoon characters she alleges she has met in real life – and she's going to name names!** In another text, he related the latest scandal in the block: **Apartment 6's teenage son has been caught redirecting all the food delivery drones to his apartment for a party he was planning.** And in the same message, he related the details of the breakdown of the marriage in Apartment 36. **Josie found Neil in bed with Rita from Apartment 70. Josie didn't mind that so much, but when she saw Rita was wearing her best negligee, an anniversary present from Neil, she went berserk.**

Scrolling through these messages, Colette smiles, *Jim sounds like he was a humorous man,* she decides. In another entry he was musing about conditions at the vast news conglomerate which he presided over:

I was running so late for a meeting the other day I had to have my dinner in the staff canteen. I hadn't been down there since I was a reporter years ago. It was still the same disgusting dump. We used to call it "Black Aggie's" after the name of the woman who ran it. It's no better now – greasy, dirty plates, food spilt on the old formica-topped tables, green, evil-smelling meat...I must do something to improve things.

Colette pauses to have a few mouthfuls of dinner before returning to the diary, she continues reading...gradually the tone of the diary became darker as the years rolled by. More and more wars were breaking out all over the world. The military elites everywhere were producing ever-more lethal computerised robot warriors and drones, programmed with one aim: to kill, no matter what, or who.

Other disturbing events were also occurring. Bands of unemployed youths, worldwide, were forming into armies, festooning themselves with lethal weapons, going on rampages through cities, destroying everything and everyone they came across, particularly attacking the robots in factories who had taken their jobs.

Another diary item makes Colette sit bolt upright. Sophie, home from her latest assignment, had written to Jim, who was himself away somewhere:

The entire electricity grid for our city has been sabotaged. Fortunately, we all have solar power for our domestic needs, but the city's transport system, our office blocks, all our infrastructure such as our water supply is computerised and depends on electric power. Can it be repaired? If not, we're in real strife. I'm beginning to think Jim and I had better leave Pacific Avenue, much as we love living here beside the sea, and go to live in our holiday place up the Mountains where at least we have our own water tank and vegetable garden, and milk from the dairy at the farm down the road."

But, Colette reads on, Sophie and Jim remained at Pacific Avenue for a year or so longer. They were still working and enjoyed their jobs. But the world was in an ever-downward spiral. One calamity after another was occurring. Nasty viruses were spreading through beleaguered cities, knocking out entire populations in Europe. Asia and America. The doctors were unable to combat these bugs and the hospitals too disorganized to be of use. In the chaos of war and upheaval no drugs could be developed to prevent or cure the terrible diseases caused by these new strains of virus. More and more cities were disrupted by computer hackers and saboteurs. Virtually nobody lived out in the countryside by then, so once a city was attacked, the entire population was under siege.

Finally, Sophie and Jim decided to leave for the Mountains. They had packed everything they wanted to take with them in a hired electric truck and were about to lock up and leave their apartment the following day, when Sophie entered a terse item into her online diary:

> **Jim received an urgent call this afternoon from the proprietor of the news corporation he works for. Jim was ordered to set off first thing tomorrow morning for Tokyo to cover a major emergency meeting between the Prime Minister of Japan and the President of China. I was distraught at the idea of him going into that lethal territory. In the night I woke up screaming: "Don't go Jim! Don't go."**
>
> **"I'll be OK," Jim comforted me. "It's only for a few days, and it'll do me good – it'll clear my mind. This desk job gets me down sometimes. It'll do me good to get out for a while."**
>
> **My outburst of fear must have been some kind of premonition, because the day after he arrived in Tokyo, I got a call once again from our proprietor, "Jim has been killed by a drone-bomber outside the Japanese parliament building." Oh Jim, my darling, darling Jim. I can't live without you. You are my whole existence.**

Colette reads on a few further entries. After a service in Jim's honour, and farewells to her friends, Sophie had set off for the Mountains in the automated electric truck she and Jim had hired to transport their goods and chattels. She planned to buy a small electric car when she got to the Mountains – she'd left their old car back in their garage at Pacific Avenue because she had to accompany the furniture in the van. She was still devastated by the dreadful turn of events, and only her natural instinct for survival, which had carried her through many dangerous assignments in the past, kept her going.

> **I'll miss the sea. I'll keep the webcam on our balcony running for as long as possible, so I can call it up and view the ocean from a distance. But most of all, I'll miss Jim dreadfully when I get up the Mountains – our long conversations there on winter evenings...cuddling up to him on freezing nights with the wind howling outside...all the memories of parties we had there...but at least there are some friends there. They do very old-fashioned, Olden Day, things like holding philosophy and history forums, where people are encouraged to speak their minds, unlike the numbing Group Think we have elsewhere nowadays. But without Jim I'll be only half a person. I'll miss him always...**

This is the last entry in the diary which Colette has found in the apartment. Perhaps Sophie had continued it when she reached the house in the Mountains?

Colette puts her head in her hands. This has been so sad to read. She knows from piecing together snippets of Big Data salvaged after the Calamity, that things had become horrendously difficult in the Northern Hemisphere by then. But now, to read this personal, tragic, account of what had happened is almost too much for Colette to bear.

I think I'll go for a walk down the beach for a while. This is all too much for me to cope with, she decides.

The beachfront at that time of night is empty. She walks under the Norfolk pines and peers down the beach to Pacific Avenue. The moon is rising, not quite full, scattering diamonds across the ocean. The building where Sophie and Jim had lived is just a tiny dot in the distance at the other end of the beach but

AFTER THE ULTIMATE VIRUS

Colette thinks she can make out the flames of a fire. She smiles.
Lorf must have caught enough fish for their dinner

7

RENDEZVOUS

FINALLY IT is Sunday and time for Colette's rendezvous with Marcus 460 at Pacific Avenue.

She's full of trepidation about Marcus 460's motives. She finds it almost impossible to comprehend that the Chief Administrator, of all people, is planning to join her there. Why does he want to come to Pacific Avenue? He has obviously never been there before. How should she behave in his presence? Would he still be as strict about her disobedience? Or would he just go into the building, make a quick inspection, decide that Lorf and his group must be moved on? Or what? But why would he want her to be there too?

Nevertheless, now that she has read some of her clone-mother's diary, Colette is eager to look at the apartment again, able to see Sophie and Jim going about their lives. She'd take a closer look at the kitchen to inspect those bossy appliances Sophie had mentioned and she would take with her a screwdriver this time, and some kind of chisel, so she could open the rusty filing cabinet and perhaps find other items of interest in it. And she would take a chain and padlock for the door.

It's time to catch the morning tide, so Colette packs her clothes and tools and sets off once again down the beach, the pale sand massaging her feet as she walks.

Reaching the Wire, she goes through the same rigmarole as last time, heaving her bag over to the other side of the fence, and then swimming through the surf to get around the Wire. Aware this time of the camera, she towels herself swiftly and gets dressed and hurries to the stairs leading up to Pacific Avenue. She reaches the top of the stairs and is just about to cross the road when she looks up to see Marcus 460 standing there.

She hardly recognises him. Instead of his usual dark suit and crisp white shirt, he is wearing shorts and a t-shirt and sunglasses. Despite her surprise, she notes he has really good legs.

"Hello, Colette," he greets her, and, to her amazement, he smiles.

She is further surprised to see that he is carrying a large bag and a broom.

"Let's go in and you can introduce me to Lorf," Marcus 460 says, starting to cross the road towards the garage entrance. Dazed, Colette follows him into the building. In the gloom she makes out Lorf and goes over to him.

"Lorf," she says. "I want you to meet our Chief Admin...Mr...."

Marcus cuts her short. "Hi, Marcus is my name," he says, holding out his hand and shaking Lorf's. "I've come to see where Colette's clone-mum lived."

Lorf calls over an old woman with straggly hair and only one leg.

"This is 'Azel, my wifey," he says. Hazel smiles warmly at Colette and Marcus.

"I've 'eard about youse," she says, gesturing towards Colette. "Youse come 'ere before, dunno why."

Lorf points to the corridor leading to the stairwell and Marcus indicates to Colette that they should go up at once. Colette follows him, still bewildered. He takes off his sunglasses in the gloom as they move toward the staircase.

"You go first," he tells her, "And I'll follow. And from now on, in private, please call me just Marcus. – Mr Administrator is for office use only."

Colette begins to negotiate her way through the piles of fishbones on the stairs. Halfway up, she slips on a piece of raw fish and starts to fall. Swiftly, Marcus catches hold of her arm and steadies her.

"We can't have you spraining your ankle," he says, with that same penetrating look he'd given her in his office and she feels an electric charge as he holds her arm. Then he lets go and they continue up the stairs. Reaching the front door of Apartment 2, Marcus pulls out a knife and quickly cuts the makeshift rope she had tied the door with last time.

RENDEZVOUS

"Don't worry," he says, pushing the door open. "I've brought some hinges to replace the rusty ones as well as a chain and a programmed swipe card to slip past the lock to keep the place safe when we leave. I got two swipe cards. Here's one for you."

Colette, although surprised by this offer, doesn't say anything, and shows Marcus around the apartment. Dusty as it is, it's still glamorous, and Marcus is impressed. He finds the kitchen with its ultra-modern appliances particularly fascinating.

"It's a pity there's no running water," he remarks, and a wistful expression comes over his face.

After Colette shows him the two balconies, Marcus turns to her and smiles again.

"That's some view!" he exclaims. "How about you sweep the balcony a bit with the broom I brought while I fix the door hinges and then I'll take down some of these hamburgers to Lorf and his mates? I think they need some meat protein for a change. instead of all that fish. I'll just get that little table and the chairs out and when I come back we can sit down on the balcony and have some lunch. I have some important things to discuss with you."

Leaving Colette to clean up the balcony, Marcus deftly replaces the rusty hinges and departs, putting one bag containing what she assumes are more hamburgers on the table, and taking the other bag down to the motley crew of clone rejects down in the garage. He is quite a long time away, and Colette, having swept the worst of the dust off the balcony, sits down on one of the chairs and tries to get a grip on events. *What does Marcus want to discuss with me?* She finds herself now referring to him as Marcus, not the Chief Administrator. *Why is he so different from the Marcus I have encountered in his office?* She tries to make sense of it all.

Finally Marcus comes back. "I sat down a while with Lorf and some of them," he explains. "Once you get over their grotesque appearances, and their filthy clothes, and the stench, they're a good bunch. They must have led a hell of a life, scrounging for some kind of an existence. Some of them seem quite intelligent, though there are some very rough ones. The women are pretty rough too, but one or two seemed quite gentle – Lorf's Hazel, for example. – and pleasant and surprisingly normal, apart from the fact that they don't have all their limbs.

"I noticed a lot of them had a bad eye infection. I think you mentioned that too. Next time I come I'll bring them some ointment."

'Next time' he comes! Colette is more surprised than ever.

Marcus opens the other package he has brought. First, he takes out a little battery-powered heating plate and puts it on the table. Then he opens a small box and takes out a plate of savory-smelling rice and some succulent grilled spare ribs. Finally he produces two wine glasses and a bottle of red wine.

"That's the best I could cook up in my little kitchen," he says, unscrewing the top of the wine bottle and pouring some of the ruby liquid into the two glasses.

"This is a very special old wine, four gold medals, salvaged by our crew from one of the top hotels in the old city. Cheers"

"Cheers," replies Colette, beginning to relax and enjoy this odd occasion, and they clink glasses.

As they eat the first course, Marcus begins to speak. He looks solemn for a moment.

"You must be wondering what this is all about," he begins. "I have been keeping an eye on you for some time and I now believe you have that vital spark in you that I'm looking for in the people in our Colony.

"I've already gathered a few like-minded souls around me and I want to invite you to join us. I need people who are prepared to flout the rules if there's a good reason to do so.

"The reason is that this Colony is in deep trouble."

Colette stiffens. "What do you mean?" she asks.

"I mean exactly what I say: the Colony is in deep trouble. We have managed to salvage the wreckage of the human race from what might have been total annihilation. We have pulled together a tiny society which functions satisfactorily. We have achieved spectacular feats in reconstructing what we have of a civilization, salvaging what we could from the Best of Times before The Calamity and the Ultimate Virus. We're feeding everyone, increasing our population, even enjoying life on this lovely stretch of beach. But…" Marcus pauses.

"But?" asks Colette encouragingly.

RENDEZVOUS

"But we have become a colony of walking zombies," Marcus declares, turning his face to look out over the ocean, his hands gripping the arms of his chair.

"Tell me what you mean by zombies," urges Colette, "because I suspect I know what you're getting at."

"Well," Marcus goes on, "we're burying our heads in the sand. We're not facing up to the real challenges that loom. OK, we have been through traumatic times, and it's only natural that we have crept into a safe sanctuary, and we *have* got things running quite well, but we're wandering around in a false dream. We're living off things salvaged from The Best of Times, but we don't make anything new. Things are starting to wear out and break. The old batteries can't be re-charged many more times. We're starting to run out of toilet paper, for chrissake. We need to generate more power than just what the solar panels produce. wind power's no use to us – there's no grid to feed it into, for one thing, and manufacturing their rotablades is far beyond us anyway.

"We've skimmed the best of everything that we scrounged out of the old shops and warehouses.

"We need to realise that we're living in a false paradise. We have no form of government apart from a bureaucracy which is fast gobbling up everyone. We have completely lost any spirit of enterprise. We're no longer pioneers – we're suspended in a dream. And if we don't fight our way out of the dream soon, we are doomed."

Marcus leans forward for a moment and takes Colette's hand. "I need your help," he pleads. "Help me get things moving again. Help me to set things right."

Colette feels a thrill as his hand touches hers. She's both startled and moved by what Marcus is saying.

"Yes," she replies. "I do know what you mean. And yes, I would like to help. I know from my own experience how vapid everyone is. Nobody seems to care about anything- apart from what fun they're planning for the next Sunday, and what they're going to wear. They're like children! They don't want to know anything about the past. I've tried to interest my friends in the past, but they simply don't want to know. They *are* walking zombies!"

Marcus throws his hands in the air. "Great!" he almost shouts. "I'd hoped you would understand. I need to tell you so much more about what I and my helpers are doing. But the tide will be turning soon, and you still have to swim back today. I'll make sure we have a better arrangement in future about how to get you here."

"Oh, I don't mind swimming," Colette replies. "But before I go, could you please explain to me why you are so different from how I thought you were? Everyone is terrified of you. You are the great ogre…and yet…you don't seem like that after all. In fact," she pauses, "I could even get to like you!"

Marcus smiles his quick smile again.

"Yes Colette, I'm not surprised you're puzzled. You see, to have got to where I have reached – the top rung of a very slippery ladder – has not been an easy task. I have had to assume a persona, a disguise. You see, I have a great deal of enemies, including some of the new generation of Elders, who do not like me one little bit and are doing their best to get rid of me. They're like serpents in our Garden of Eden. I have had to inch my way up through the ranks of the bureaucracy to reach the top. It has not been an easy job. I am watched wherever I go in the Colony. My office has spy cameras beamed on me all the time. Even to get here today I had to take a very circuitous route. But at least there aren't any cameras here. I'll tell you more next time I see you, but in the meantime, keep your eyes and ears open and your mouth shut, which I know you will. We are living in dangerous times and I need loyal friends.

"Now let's get you ready for your swim back home."

8

SUPERMARKET

OVER THE next few days, Colette finds herself thinking a lot about what Marcus has told her. It is as if the scales have been lifted from her eyes. She is suddenly seeing everything – the Colony, her job, her friends, her whole life – in a different perspective. *I, too, have been a walking zombie,* she concludes. *"I've been living in a dream, a nice, comfortable but boring dream. But like Marcus says, we can't go on for much longer this way. We must get some basic things sorted out, otherwise, we won't survive too much longer.*

In her office, Colette throws herself into her work with new zeal, realizing now that it is very important to find out as much as possible about the world before The Calamity. She wants to sort the chaff from the wheat, to find out what had been good in the old civilisation and what had caused it to turn so worryingly bad. *We can certainly learn some lessons from the past*, she thinks. *But will human nature be able to change?*

Colette is also delving deeper into her clone-mother, Sophie's, past. Turning back to the beginning of Sophie's diary, she comes across an entry about going to the supermarket – not so much to buy – she could order everything online to be delivered – but to *feel* the latest goods on display. The 3D holograms on TV were a marvellous way to *see* things, but to actually *feel* and *touch* them was more satisfying. And going to the supermarket occasionally meant you could bump into your neighbours and friends.

"On my next afternoon off I must go and visit the Supermarket exhibit in the Mall Museum," Colette determines, turning to Rodney, who is sitting with her over lunch. "Would you like to come with me to the Supermarket exhibit in the Mall Museum" she asks him.

43

AFTER THE ULTIMATE VIRUS

Rodney has been scraping the bottom of his soup bowl in a desperate attempt to get the last drop. His 187.96-centimeter frame, honed by his regular trips to the gym, craves kilojoules. He looks at her in surprise. "Why would that interest me?" he asks her. "Wasn't that all a long time ago?"

"OK. Never mind," she replies. "I'll go by myself."

She calls up all the Big Data on supermarkets she can locate and soon she's absorbed and credulous, finding it hard to grasp the phenomenon. A supermarket? A large store, part of a chain of stores, packed with thousands of items, mostly packaged in brightly-coloured packets and cans – amazing! The Colony, by contrast, has only the one shop, a second-hand clothing shop. As Sophie had mentioned in her diary, the people in those days sure were spoilt!

Colette determines to visit the display supermarket in the Mall up the Junction on her day off. She could legitimately claim the visit because it is part of her current work project. On Wednesday afternoon she catches the electric bus and gets out at the Junction Mall, locating the Supermarket exhibit on the digital map at the entrance. It is on the first floor, up the stairs – the old escalators don't function nowadays because they eat up too much precious power. At the entrance to the supermarket exhibit, Colette slips her employment-rank ID card into the slot. It registers approval of her Level 2 status which guarantees she is old enough not to be swayed by the luxury goods she would see inside the exhibit.

Despite her research into the phenomenon, Colette is unprepared for the impact of the real thing – or at least a simulacrum of a real supermarket. Just before The Calamity, some far-sighted museum employees, sensing impending doom, had decided that a supermarket was so quintessentially an icon of The Best of Times that a copy of one should be preserved for posterity. As far as possible, those designers used real cans and boxes from a real supermarket, only resorting to plastic models for items of food that would otherwise have rotted and gone bad.

Bright, jangly piped music greets Colette's ears as she enters. A row of automated wire trolleys awaits her, ready to guide her through the display. Glaring lights shine down from neon strips above a series of aisles; she has never seen such lights before. She looks down the aisles at endless shelves containing row-after-row of jars and cans and cartons displaying their contents. "Pasta", "Biscuits, "Bread" "Cereal" announces her trolley as it moves along the first aisle. Next comes the tea and coffee – every type of blend and flavour, all packed in alluring boxes, waiting to jump off the shelves into the trolley of some housewife in The Best of Times. Signs announcing "AS SEEN ON TV" and "BARGAIN PRICE!" or "PRICES DOWN, DOWN, DOWN" force Colette, unaccustomed to this blatant sales pitch, to avert her eyes.

The trolley turns into the next aisle. There, Colette sees a large cabinet which looks as if it were covered in ice – fake ice, she discovers when she touches it. Inside the cabinet is a cornucopia of fish and cold meats, sliced and displayed on serving boards. Colette has never seen such a variety of meats before. In the next aisle is soup. She makes a mental list of the 25 different brands of chicken soup stacked on the shelves. It comes in concentrated, condensed, with corn, with roast chicken pieces, with noodles, without noodles, with mushrooms... an endless selection. *How confusing!* she thinks, *we just have one type of chicken soup.* Then came dental products and cosmetics and she marvels at the range of shampoos to suit every type of hair. *It makes my trusty organic shampoo seem very dull.* Next, the trolley takes her around to the soft drinks area where every flavour and combination of tastes are on offer: pineapple and orange, lemon and lime; passionfruit and mango, diet or sugared, fizzy or flat...Colette's eyes swivel from one shelf to the next. After surveying the desserts and yoghurts, the ice-creams and jellies, she feels she's got the message.

It is all so over-the-top it positively frightens her, and she hurries out of the supermarket exhibit and back down the corridor, passing by another exhibition shop whose windows display models wearing white diaphanous lace dresses with net-veiled headwear. Puzzled, she goes over to the display notice and learns the dresses are wedding dresses, ready for a bride on the day of her marriage. Colette is fascinated. Marriage! She now knows that Sophie and Jim had been married, but the concept of marriage is so foreign to her. Couples in the Colony sometimes lived together for a while, and a few had long-term relationships, but, living, as most of them did, in small, cramped apartments, the Colonists usually found co-habiting with another person was too claustrophobic. Few couples stayed together for long, and the idea of wearing a long white dress with a veil on one's wedding day is something completely beyond Colette's imagination.

She takes the bus home, looking out at the Colony as she passes by the apartment blocks near where she lives. *I'm glad I live a much simpler life*, she thinks as she alights from the bus and goes home to her simple evening meal delivered to her hatch from the Colony kitchen.

Next morning in her office she finds a note tucked carefully out of sight under her compudule. It says simply: *7pm tonight. Meeting at my place. Taxi will pick you up corner of Esplanade.*

9

TO THE GULLY HOUSE

THAT EVENING Colette starts to find something
appropriate to wear to the meeting at Marcus's house. She doesn't
have much choice – she could either wear her red dress or her
black-and-white striped dress. She chooses the red one, slips it on,
brushes her hair and sets off down the Esplanade to wait for her
cab on the corner. On the dot it arrives and slides its door open for
her to jump in. Then Colette is stumped. She doesn't know where
Marcus lives. Did he live up the Hill, "Toff's Hill", as some of the
Colony's young ones dubbed it? Most likely. But Colette doesn't
have to worry, the cab announces it is taking her to a meeting not
far away and it tells her they will arrive by 7pm. So she sits back
and tries to relax as the cab travels along the rest of the Esplanade
and then stops in front of the big gate in the Wire. The gate
clicks open automatically, letting the cab through. It must
have been programmed to do that, thinks Colette.

Then they drive up a rather bumpy road into an alien
landscape she can only dimly see though the night air; it is
completely unfamiliar. She begins to feel a little nervous,
concerned that here she is, being taken by an automatic cab,
outside the Colony where nobody is allowed to go – in the night.
Empty, boarded-up shops flash by. There are no street lights, so
she can't see much. Then they turn off the main street and drive
along an even more rutted and bumpy road with little boarded-up
houses on either side. Finally, they turn again and start travelling
down a sloping road through a gully of eucalypts and enormous
fern trees, past large, deserted beach houses submerged in foliage,
until they reach what seems to be a little plateau. She can see a
light shining from a dwelling on a hill, and then she is alarmed
when a cow wanders across the road right in front of the cab. They
swerve past it and finally approach the light, and Colette manages

to see a small, old wooden, two-storey house with a front veranda. The house, she observes, as they draw closer, is painted yellow, and there is an old cane sofa on the veranda. The bright light she has seen is on the wall next to the front door, and more light shines through coloured glass flowers at the top of the door. So this is where Marcus lives – Colette is surprised. She had imagined that because he is the Chief Administrator of the Colony he would have a big house somewhere up on the Hill, like the houses the descendants of the Elders live in. But not only is this house a long way away from the Hill's mansions which are behind high walls with wrought-iron gates closed across gravel drives, this little house is outside the Colony Wire, located, as far as she can calculate, two beaches south of the Colony Beach. Marcus continually surprises her. The cab pulls in front of a little flight of steps leading to the veranda and the front door. Colette gets out and goes to the door where she finds an old-style doorbell pull-string. She tugs it and soon the door is flung open and Marcus is standing there, with a room full of people behind him.

"Hello, Colette," Marcus greets her, "welcome to the Gully Group. We call ourselves that because we meet in my Gully. Come and meet everyone. I think you'll already know some of them."

Marcus takes Colette around the group, introducing them to her and explaining what their expertise is.

"You'll know William, of course," says Marcus. "He looks after all the computers. He and his team are vital. William is Chief IT Officer in the Gully Group.

William smiles at Colette. "Yes," he replies quietly. "I do know Colette." *Yes,* Colette nodded, *we certainly have met over Sophie's disc.*

Next, Marcus draws up a bespectacled young woman from the sofa where she has been sitting. "This is Alice, she's awesome on legal matters. She's the Group's Legal Officer." Colette hasn't met her before and assumes she must work in a back room in one of the storage libraries in the Colony. Alice smiles shyly at Colette, her dark eyes gleaming through her spectacles. *She looks like a lawyer*, notes Colette.

"Now we come to Charlie. He's an engineer in the Colony Army and is twiddling his thumbs with not enough to do any more.

He's going to be mighty useful if we manage to get things moving in the Colony. I call him our Power Chief. He knows all about electricity and fuel." Colette looks at Charlie's masterful forearms and broad, cheerful face. *Yes, he certainly exuded energy.*

Next came Simon. "Simon doesn't look like a farmer, but he already is one," says Marcus, turning to a slim young man with dark, short-cropped hair, "He works in the Department of Agriculture, but he also runs the little dairy and poultry farm down here in our gully. Simon is Head of Agriculture in the Gully Group."

"My cab nearly ran into one of your cows on the way here!" Colette remarks, and Simon laughs. "Old Bessie can take care of herself," he replies "But she doesn't know what a taxi is. She sees so few of them. She associates all vehicles with the arrival of feed."

Marcus moves on to introduce Colette to Suyen, a slightly Asian-looking girl who is wearing a navy-blue jumpsuit. "Suyen is our Campaign Manager. She will help us win the election, when it comes," says Marcus.

Election? Colette is confused. She hasn't heard anything about an election. The Colony doesn't have elections – they happened back in the Olden Days and in The Best of Times, not now.

"And, finally, this is Phil. He's our Chief of Housing. He already works in the Department of Accommodation and knows the situation back-to-front. Something of a revolution in housing in the Colony needs to happen, and Phil will be in charge of it," Marcus says, putting his hand on Phil's shoulder.

"Now," Marcus announces, "I want to put Colette in charge of Communications. She works in the Department of Big Data Verification and is brilliant at digging out and analyzing information – and making sense of it. Would you agree to helping in that capacity, Colette?"

Colette nods, "I'd be honoured to."

"We still need someone to look after Sport and Recreation, and someone else to be in charge of Health. I have my eye on two possible contenders and I'll let you know about them soon. And further down the track we will need an Exploration leader and a Manufacturing chief. But that can wait a little while.

"Now it's time for a bit of a planning session, so let's go into the dining room for that."

Marcus goes to the head of a long dining table and stands while the others come in and sit down. *Everyone in the room is friendly and relaxed, but respectful of Marcus.* Colette notes

Marcus starts to speak. "We must wake up and get moving, or else the human race – us – cannot survive. As far as we know, we are it. There doesn't seem to be anyone else "out there" – no-one in Melbourne or Brisbane or the other cities has contacted us, let alone anyone from further afield, not even any Chinese people, despite their population billions and worldwide influence before The Calamity. But they are a resilient and resourceful race and some of them are bound to pop up before long. We must work out how to trade with them. In the past, our country tended to still rely on what the bigger countries overseas did. But now it's totally up to us. We can shape the future the way we want it. And if we're clever, we can learn from past mistakes and avoid repeating them. We live in a beautiful country. We have missed the worst of The Calamity. It's time to get cracking."

The Gully Group claps in approval. Then Marcus continues:

"We know we are up against a phalanx of die-hard conservatives, indeed, latter day Fascists, led by one sector of the Elders, who regard me as a dangerous radical – a traitor to the State in fact. They are working to get rid of me as Chief Administrator, and if we don't look out, they will succeed. They have control of the administration's internal mail and CCTV system and they spy on my every move. We have to be ultra-careful about what we do, say, or text." He stops and looks around the group.

"The latest news I've learnt is that they are going to spring an election on the Colony, its first-ever election. As descendants of the original Elders, they have assumed their mantle of control and now they have cunningly resuscitated the old concept of Democracy, but it's fake Democracy, aimed at killing off any opposition. and an election is a ruse to beat us all into submission. We have to find out when this election is to be held, and we need to work mighty fast to win."

Marcus pauses for a moment, and everyone claps enthusiastically, urging him to continue.

TO THE GULLY HOUSE

"One particularly worrying thing the Elders are plotting to do if they win the Election is that they're planning to ensure that people of Caucasian ancestry are not permitted to mix with other 'inferior' races. The Elders are planning to set up "ethnic cleansing" – like Hitler's Nazis did. Though I suspect it would be an uphill task because our nation was so racially-mixed before The Calamity that even though we are cloned we're all of mixed race, one way or another.

"So now," he goes on, "we need to marshal our resources, making both short-term plans and longer-term ones – in case we do manage to win. We need to open up some of the bigger houses to allow couples to live together in larger spaces; we need to start farming; we must enlarge our water supply...we must start making things...the list is endless.

He turns to Colette: "We will need you to spread the good word about our plans. Word-of-mouth will be an important factor. I know you have a large number of friends. Drop remarks here and there and see who responds, and then set up a network. We can't do a lot online because of the Elders' spy network, but subtle texts could be useful. We will also need campaign posters and leaflets and some information for our local TV news."

With that, Marcus calls an end to the meeting and opens a couple of bottles of wine.

Colette looks at her watch and sees that it is getting late and she doesn't want to be spotted coming home in a cab at an ungodly hour. She tells Marcus she thinks she'd better go.

"I'll summon a cab," he says, pulling out his pocket phone. "Say goodbye and I'll come out with you to wait for the cab on the veranda."

Outside in the cold night air, Colette turns to Marcus, "That was an impressive meeting," she begins. "You handled it very well and everyone is keen. But what's all this about an election?"

"It could be very soon," Marcus replies, sitting down on the sofa with her. "And this is where I hope you can be of immediate help. Tomorrow evening there's a party up the Hill which I would like you to attend. It is being held by Karla, a very good and old friend. In fact, when I was quite a young man, Karla, who has always had a penchant for young men, took me under her wing. We had a long affair and she taught me a great deal about politics

– and life. She is now with Harold, her long-term partner, who used to be in charge of the Colony's finances – such as they were – and allocation of resources, before he retired. Karla and I have remained close friends. She knows everybody and has inside knowledge of politics in the Colony. Unfortunately, even she hasn't been able to find out the proposed date for the election. So now I'm relying on you – with her help. I will ask Karla to introduce you at her party to the key members of the conspirators' group, particularly Alistair, their leader. If you could inveigle your way into that group and gain their confidence, you might be able to learn some interesting things – in particular: when they plan to spring that election.

"Unfortunately, for very good reasons that you will understand, I can't appear to know you at the party. Karla might even introduce you to me!"

Colette quivers in anticipation. "What can I talk to them about?" she asks. "What kinds of things are they interested in?"

"Nazi Germany is one of their favourite topics," replies Marcus with a soft laugh. "I know you've studied that regime as part of your job. Brush up on your facts and figures and try to bring up the subject somehow. That would immediately appeal to them."

Then he turns and looked at her carefully. "What is your relationship with Rodney?" he asks. Colette is surprised at the question.

"Well," she replies. "If you want the truth, I've broken up with him, but I haven't had the heart to break the news to him yet. We have been more or less a couple for the past two years. It was convenient for both of us. – we could go out to movies and other Colony entertainments together. He's very kind, but we aren't 'in love', or at least I'm not – though we do have sex – like most other couples in the Colony 'love' doesn't come into it. In fact, I think he would be happier with my friend, Melanie – she'd be more relaxing for him. I tend to get concerned about things, but he doesn't want to discuss them."

"Good," says Marcus with a faint smile. "I'm thinking of inviting him to take on the task of organising Sport and Recreation. I think he'd be good at that, don't you?"

TO THE GULLY HOUSE

"Yes," agrees Colette. "You can rely on him. He's very trustworthy."

Seeing the cab coming down the road towards them, Colette starts to rise from the sofa. "Would anyone else like to share my cab back?" she asks.

"No," says Marcus, rising too. "It's not good for any of the Gully Group to be seen with other members. I make sure the cabs taking back the others drop them off at different points around the Colony, and at different times."

Marcus takes Colette's hand and helps her into the cab.

"Goodnight, and good luck tomorrow evening, I look forward to hearing what transpires. A cab will pick you up from your building at 6pm. It will take about eight minutes to reach Karla's house up The Hill. You'll have to get out at the front gate – cabs can't cope with the loose gravel on her driveway." And he leans down and kisses her gently on the forehead before the cab prepares to move on.

"I hope we can meet again at Number 2, Pacific Avenue very soon," he says as the cab door slides shut.

10

AT KARLA'S

ONE THOUGHT dominates her mind: when Colette wakes up next morning: what on earth to wear to the party that evening? It is obviously going to be a slap-up event, but she really doesn't have anything to wear. Before her breakfast arrives, she begins rummaging through her wardrobe in a desperate attempt to find something that is even remotely elegant. Finally, she takes out her black-and-white striped dress. It is very simple and quite long. Maybe if she found a necklace, it would pass muster. Having resolved this burning question, she sits down to her breakfast and begins thinking about the events of the night before at Marcus's house. *He certainly seems to be on top of matters*, she decides. *And he demonstrated the ability to be in command while keeping everyone on side. He obviously has a very good mind and has thought a great deal about the future of the Colony. But would he be able to muster the numbers in time to win the election? How much time would he have before the election?* Colette realises her mission tonight will be crucial for planning the Gully Group's campaign. *And he kissed me on the forehead!* As she drinks her coffee, she decides to get to work very early so she can bone up on her research into Nazi history, as Marcus had requested.

Arriving at the office, she asks her compudule to call up all the relevant files she has researched on the Nazis. Then she starts to read. She doesn't want to delve too deeply into the murky politics and activities of the Nazi regime, so, instead, she concentrates on their art, it being a safer topic for discussion at a cocktail party anyway, she feels. She recalls how repulsed she had been by the way the Nazis had taken Greek and Roman art forms and transformed them into sickly sentimental works, but she did recall their striking poster designs. She spends the whole morning re-reading her notes until she feels she can't bear any more.

AT KARLA'S

Closing down her compudule, she goes down to the staff canteen where she joins Rodney and a group of friends. Colette feels a bit guilty about Rodney. In the heady time since her first encounter with Marcus, which seems ages ago now, she has been living in a different realm and she has neglected Rodney somewhat of late. He is a dear, and she is very fond of him, but... She sees him talking to Melanie, a pretty girl with dark curly hair and a sweet smile. *Maybe Rodney would be happier with someone like Melanie?*

After lunch, Colette returns to her office, but she can't concentrate on anything. The impending party is at the forefront of her mind. How is she to get that information Marcus so badly needs? It seems an impossible task. Because she had started work so early, she is able to leave the office at 4pm, and she decides to go down to the beachfront and get some fresh air. A strong southerly is blowing and the whitecaps are dancing on the waves as far as the horizon. A lone fisherman stands on the sand, the rising tide lapping around his ankles, and seagulls wheel above him.

She walks back to her building and opens the door to her apartment. To her surprise, there is a large white box on the dining table, and two smaller boxes beside it. She goes over to the largest box and lifts its lid. Inside is a note saying *"Blue, to match those eyes of yours. M"*. Under the note is a shimmering, full-length blue evening dress. Colette takes it out and holds it against herself. It is simple and elegant. The shoulder straps are encrusted with clear crystal beads. It's stunning. Then she opens the second box and finds inside a pair of exquisite silver sandals. In the third box is a simple silver choker necklace.

"Oh my god!" Colette exclaims out loud. "Marcus thinks of everything."

She goes to the bathroom and has a shower and after towelling herself dry she carefully puts on the dress. It fits her slender figure perfectly. She looks in the mirror and sees a transformed image of herself and decides to coil her hair above her neck. Then she tries on the sandals. Another perfect fit. She starts to teeter around in them – she's never worn high heels before – and decides she'd better practise walking around the room. Soon she is twirling around freely. She puts on the necklace and checks herself in the mirror.

"March on, Colette," she orders herself. *"Into battle!"* Checking her watch, she pulls her old coat over her dress in the hope nobody will notice her and goes down to the front of the building where her cab is waiting. It drives up The Hill past the big mansions, some of them with lights glowing, others empty, as they have been for decades, and then turns into a side street. Halfway along the street, the cab pulls up at a pair of imposing double gates set in a high stone fence. Colette takes off her coat and instructs the cab to come back at 9.30pm and to bring her coat back too. The cab blinks a green light as she gets out. A young man wearing a uniform is standing at the gate.

"Welcome," he says. "Please come through this side gate and take the path beside the gravel drive. Lovely sandals like yours can't cope with a gravel drive." Colette follows him through into the large garden behind the stone wall.

Karla greets her at the door. Colette sees a woman of about 50 with silver-blond hair done in a chignon, wearing an elegant off-the-shoulder, silver-grey gown.

"Come in, my dear," says Karla in a melodic voice. "I've heard quite a lot about you."

Inside, they pass a wide staircase leading up to a higher floor. Karla pushes open a pair of cedar double doors and leads Colette into a large, softly-lit room full of men in dinner suits and women in elegant gowns. Glasses tinkle and a waiter with a tray is passing around drinks.

"Let me introduce you to some of my neighbours," Karla says, taking Colette's elbow and guiding her towards a group of men, all of them silver-haired or balding, standing in front of a marble fireplace.

"Gentlemen," announces Karla, "I'd like you to meet Colette, the star of the Department of Big Data Verification."

The men cease talking and turn to look at Colette, standing there, stunningly, in her blue dress.

"Colette, meet Alistair," says Karla, and Alistair, a tall, dignified and slightly portly man in his sixties, steps forward and takes Colette's hand.

My dear," he purrs, eyeing her up-and-down. "I'm delighted to meet someone whom Karla describes as a star. High praise indeed."

Colette, recognising Alistair as the fabled chief of the Elders, replies, "She is flattering me," and smiles.

"And what do you do in your work for the Department?" asks Alistair, deciding to prolong the introduction before Colette is introduced to the rest of the group.

"I do research into the old political regimes and lifestyles of former civilisations," replies Colette. "Currently I'm studying the Third Reich in Germany and finding it absolutely fascinating."

"My dear, that is a subject close to my heart!" exclaims Alistair, still holding Colette's hand. "We must discuss the subject more in a minute.

"But first, let me take over from Karla and I'll introduce you to my friends."

Karla drifts off to attend to her other guests, leaving Colette with Alistair and the other men, whom he introduces as Rupert, Lionel, Aubrey, and Montgomery – all names of Elders she has heard about.

"Now, my dear," says Alistair, beaming down at her. "What aspect of German life has tickled your fancy most?"

Colette is careful. She doesn't want to mention Hitler, so she smiles again and says she is particularly impressed by the Nazi's sense of graphic design.

"I love some of their posters," she says, referring not to the horrific caricatures of Jews she has seen in some of them, but to the ones where the graphic design was excellent.

"And their swastika, what an image!" agrees Alistair with a confidential chuckle, "And we know who was the genius who came up with that logo!"

"Yes," agrees Colette. "That *was* a stroke of genius." The group clusters around her, mentioning the painting of Adolf Zeigler and other painters favoured by the Nazis.

"Wonderful work," murmurs Montgomery, smoothing his silver moustache.

"I beg to differ there," Colette says boldly, "They took the Greek and Roman ideals because they felt the Greek statues embodied purity of race, but they over-sentimentalised them.

Their paintings were a reversion to an old-fashioned weak sentimentalism."

"You're a woman after my own heart!" exclaims Alistair. "Their graphic art was superb, but their painting leaves a lot to be desired. Their sculpture was much more robust – the works of Hans Schweitzer, "Thor's Hammer" as he was known, for example. But I do get tired of all that monumental stuff. Of course, I have a soft spot for Leni Riefenstahl – her filming of the 1936 Olympics is an art form in itself. But their graphic art is what I'm keen on. Come, my dear, and sit down with me and we can discuss this subject more. Would you like another drink?"

Colette replies that she is fine for the moment and Alistair puts his arm around her waist and guides her over to a sofa in the corner of the rom. Colette glances sideways as they move and catches sight of Marcus on the other side of the room. He looks elegant in his dinner suit and is talking to a group of men and woman who are laughing at something he has just said. He shows no sign of recognising her.

All the while, Colette has been experiencing a strange sensation. She feels as if she's been in this house, in this room, before. It all seems strangely familiar to her: the brocade-covered mahogany chairs, the chandeliers, the Persian rugs spread out over polished boards. She feels completely at home here, which gives her courage to deal with Alistair and his friends.

Alistair continues to probe Colette about her knowledge of the Nazi regime, moving slowly towards the politics. She is beginning to feel trapped, when Karla fortunately comes over and suggests that Colette should be allowed to meet some of the other people at the party.

"You can't monopolise this pretty girl, Alistair," jokes Karla. "Let me take her away from you now and you can reclaim her later, after supper."

Relieved, Colette smiles back regretfully at Alistair as Karla draws her up and starts to lead her to the other side of the room.

"We most certainly will talk again later," promises Alistair, eyeing Colette up-and-down again as she turns and leaves.

"Yes," promises Colette. "Later…"

AT KARLA'S

Next, Karla introduces her to the group which had been enjoying something Marcus has said. Karla introduces her to some of the women in the group and then she turns to Marcus.

"Marcus, this is Colette. She works in one of your departments."

Marcus looks at Colette and replies.

"Oh yes," he says. "I think I've seen you somewhere before. Which department are you in?"

Colette replies, and Marcus then asks her if she is enjoying her work there.

"Yes, very much, Sir," she says.

"Oh, that's good," he replies. "I'm glad they're keeping you busy down there." And he turns back to the other guests while Karla steers Colette to meet others in the room, including her husband, Harold, a distinguished-looking man in an embroidered dinner jacket, who is obviously not part of Alistair's group of cronies. "I'll see that you return to Alistair's circle after supper," Karla says quietly, and Colette nods in thanks.

Supper is served in another room which opens through double doors from the front room. The candle-lit table is laden with platters of food, the like of which Colette has never before seen, and yet, somehow, she knows exactly how the food will taste. This feeling of *deja vu* haunts her. There is caviar and *fois gras*, oysters marinated in white wine… Colette wonders where this exotic food could have come from. The caviar and *fois gras* have probably come from the stores of goods removed from the shop shelves by the Army after The Calamity. Despite its age, the food looked quite fresh – no doubt kept in ultra-bionic-refrigerators.

A dessert course is brought in by the waiter, and delicate English porcelain plates are distributed for the guests to help themselves to stewed peaches in brandy and a mountain of ice-cream sprinkled with passionfruit juice, and stewed apricots set in blocks of ice.

Just before the guests prepare to move back to the front room, Colette asks Karla if she could visit the bathroom. Karla takes her to the hall and starts to guide her, but Colette waives her aside. "It's fine," she replies, "I think I know where it is."

"Alright," says Karla, a little surprised, "but if you get lost give me a holler."

Strangely, Colette finds the bathroom straight away. And it, too, looks familiar with its dish of *pot pourri* near the window, its old-fashioned lavatory with a chain-pull cistern, and next door, an old white enamel bathtub standing on four curved iron legs.

Returning to the party, Colette sees Alistair making a beeline for her.

"Come, my dear," he says, "We all want a word with you." By "we" he is obviously referring to the other Elders Colette has met earlier.

They have commandeered the sofa and several armchairs around the fireplace, which holds a large vase of burgundy-petalled waratahs, a suitable summer replacement for a roaring fire.

They are passing around a box of cigars, once again purloined from the central stores, and Colette, fascinated, watches them starting to smoke. She had seen photographs of people such as Winston Churchill, smoking cigars, but she's never seen anyone in the Colony light even a cigarette, let alone a cigar. Alistair offers her a glass of port, but she declines. "I find port a little heavy," she lies, not having ever tasted a drop of port in her life. She notices the group is imbibing the port liberally and she also notices that the drink is starting to go to their cheeks, if not their heads.

It soon becomes obvious that Alistair has been discussing her after Karla had taken her off to meet other guests. After a few light-hearted references to Nazi uniforms being so stylish, the conversation, this time led by Montgomery, turns serious. They then talk about the Colony and the need to maintain strict discipline – as Hitler had done. Colette hears ideas being expressed which are so fascist, they might indeed have come out of Goebbels or Goering's own mouths. She notices that Alistair says very little, letting Montgomery, Aubrey, and the others warm to their fascist theme. However, he finally speaks:

"My dear," says Alistair conspiratorially, "we have something we'd like to discuss with you."

"Oh?" inquires Colette.

AT KARLA'S

"Yes, we sense in you a kindred spirit. You are so young, yet, unlike all the other young people in the Colony, you appreciate the finer things in life, in civilisation. We are presently fighting to save our Colony from outright ruin. A bunch of loony radicals are trying to take over the place, trying to undermine what our ancestors, the Elders, strove so hard to create, to build, out of the ruins of a corrupt and destructive world. We believe we will win this battle, but we do need younger people to understand our cause and to vote for us in the coming election.

"An election? We've never had an election. I didn't know we were going to have one," Colette says, trying to sound genuinely surprised.

"Oh, yes, my dear. We have been forced into taking this drastic step," replies Alistair, pumping the arm of the sofa with his hand.

Colette almost asks when the election will be held, but she holds her tongue – she doesn't want to look too obviously interested in such a matter.

"So how are you going to appeal to the citizens of the Colony," she asks.

"Well," chimes in Montgomery, "we know we have all the older people on side. They like things as they are, and they certainly don't want change. They don't want to upset the applecart."

"Oh," says Colette. "And what about the younger people?"

"Well this is where you come in," says Alistair, leaning forward and taking her hand. "We want your help. You would be able to appeal to the younger generation and show them how important it is to conserve what civilisation we have managed to salvage from the wreckage of the Calamity.

"You could go on TV and look attractive and tell the young ones about style and elegance and the kind of things we have discussed this evening. Then you could subtly insert into their minds what dangers are in store for the Colony if they were to vote for that mad radical, Marcus," and he turns and gazes across the room at Marcus for a moment. "You'd wow them," he adds, using an old-fashioned piece of slang. "You would be our poster girl!"

Colette looks at Alistair inquiringly. "But when is this all going to happen? I have my work to do and I don't have much spare time."

"It wouldn't take up too much of your time," Alistair assures her, still holding her hand. "We plan to spring the election on the community on …" and he looks at his watch. "On Saturday the 24th of December to be precise, the day before Christmas Day. So will you join us? Will you help us woo the youth vote?"

Colette hesitates. She certainly doesn't want to agree to anything Alistair wants her to do, but neither does she want to reveal any lack of support for him – otherwise he might smell a rat.

"Your offer certainly bears thinking about," she replies smiling again and trying to look enthusiastic. "Let me sleep on it. I'll tell you in a day or so once I've had time to sort out my work schedule. Indeed, I must dash off home now. I have an early morning assignment at the information depot.

"It has been really lovely to meet you and your friends tonight," she goes on, "and to be able to talk about the Third Reich art in particular. Could you give me your contact details and I'll be in touch?"

With that, Colette gently disentangles her hand from Alistair's and gets up, turning to the others on the couch and bidding them farewell. Montgomery blows a little kiss and Alistair claps his hands softly.

"Goodbye, dear," he says. "I look forward to working with you soon."

Colette then goes over to Karla, explaining she has to leave, and that she has booked a cab to pick her up at 9.30 pm. Karla escorts her to the front door, pointing out that the path down to the gate is well-lit, and apologising to Colette that she has to walk to the gate because the gravel drive doesn't accommodate taxi tyres.

"Well, Colette, you were a great hit with Alistair and his cronies," jokes Karla, "Was your mission successful?"

"It was indeed," Colette replies, "Thanks to you we have the information we need. And thank you for a lovely party, it was truly enjoyable."

"You must come again," Karla says. "I know how to get in touch with you now. Good night, Colette, see you again soon."

AT KARLA'S

Colette doesn't see it, but Karla gives an approving nod at her departing figure.

Colette walks down the path to the gate, her head swimming. As she turns out of the gate into the darkened street, a shadow passes in front of her, and then a man emerges from the trees. It is Marcus.

"Colette," he says. "You were magnificent." And he puts his arms around her and kisses her on the lips gently but passionately. Colette feels that surge of electricity again and looks at Marcus.

"I know the date of the Election," she begins.

"Don't talk about elections now," he says, holding her tight. "I want to kiss you again."

This time, Colette is able to respond more, enjoying his second kiss even more than the first.

"Ohhh, Colette," Marcus whispers. "I need you so much."

Colette hears the sound of the cab arriving.

"I've got to go now," she says.

"I have to go now too," says Marcus. "I'll have to go around the back of the house, so nobody will notice me. I'll pretend I've been in the bathroom."

"Yes," says Colette, "There's a back door leading into a big laundry and the pantry, and then the kitchen."

Marcus looks at her curiously.

"How do you know?"

"I have no idea," says Colette "but it's true."

"And," she adds "by the way, the date for the election is Friday the 24th of December."

Marcus laughs in delight.

"Congratulations, Colette, my darling spy! Goodnight now. I'll make sure we can see each other again very soon."

And he kisses her gently and firmly one more time before helping her into her cab and waving her off.

11

ALARUMS AND EXCURSIONS

COLETTE HAS her first appointment at the Infirmary the following Monday morning. This is to familiarise her with the pregnancy process. A nurse examines her and checks her blood pressure etc, declaring her 100 per cent fit and ready for pregnancy. The process is to be followed in steps. First, she has to be inoculated to counteract the contraceptive drug she has been injected with – like all other women in the Colony – at the age of ten. This would be done today. She would now start taking pills to stimulate extra ovulation, to maximise her chances of becoming pregnant – if possible with twins – as soon as the insemination process began in six weeks' time. It is hoped she would have twins, fraternal, of course. This is the extra way to add to the population.

"What happens if I have sex with a boyfriend and get pregnant?" she asks.

The nurse frowns. "If that were to occur you would be checked and have a quick abortion. You would then be required to stay at the infirmary until your official pregnancy occurred."

Once pregnant, the nurse goes on, the young woman was permitted to return home and continue working until she reached eight-and-a-half months when she was boarded back in the Infirmary to await the birth. No breast feeding was to be allowed. The baby would be removed to the Nursery and from that time on, looked after by the Nannies. A mother was permitted to visit her baby once a week, if she wanted to. Apart from that there was no contact between mother and child.

Colette is appalled. She'd never really discussed the process with other women she knew. Most of her friends were about her age and hadn't yet been called up for pregnancy duty.

"But that's cruel!" she exclaims. "Surely the mother has the right to see her own baby!"

"The mother has done her bit for the future of the human race," the nurse intones, as if reading from a script. "Now she needs to get back into the community and pick up her old job and get on with her life. She will never know who the father of the baby is, and it is better for all if the child is reared by the Nannies – as you were when you were cloned."

"But...but...this is dreadful," Colette splutters. "No wonder so many women in the Colony suffer nervous complaints after their pregnancies. This is the elephant in the room – a scandal nobody dares to mention."

The nurse silently leads her out into the waiting room while her injection is prepared, and her pills ordered from the pharmacy. While she is sitting on the waiting room sofa Colette hears a man's voice, a very familiar voice. It is Marcus. He is laughing and joking with a young, dark-haired woman in the next room. Colette can just glimpse them through the door.

Colette stiffens. She has never heard Marcus sound so relaxed. He is laughing a lot, and before he leaves the room, he gives the woman a cuddle and kisses her on the forehead. "See you tomorrow, darling, down at my place. I'll order a taxi to pick you up," he tells her as he leaves. He walks straight to the front door of the Infirmary, not noticing Colette.

Who is this woman? Marcus obviously has a very close relationship with her. Colette finds herself trembling, recalling those passionate embraces of Friday night. *What a fool I've been to believe Marcus is especially fond of me! He obviously knows plenty of young woman as he travels around the countryside, visiting the other settlements,* Colette tells herself. *Marcus has simply been playing with me. He just wanted me to get information about the election date from those Nazis at the party.*

Back at her apartment, Colette throws herself down on the sofa and bursts into tears.

Don't be stupid, Colette, she tells herself between sobs. *You hardly know him. He's the big boss. He can get any woman he wants. Karla for example. Stop blabbering and pull yourself together. You've got to be strong to get through this pregnancy. You can't afford to cry over spilt milk.* Nevertheless, Colette is depressed and angry. *I didn't realise quite how much Marcus was affecting me,* she thinks as she eats her dinner and sits down in front of the TV.

Next day, back in her office, Colette tries to concentrate on her work. She sees Marcus in the distance, talking to her supervisor. Then he comes up to her desk.

"Good morning, Colette 850," he begins in his formal office manner. "I believe you have been researching Cold War politics lately. I have asked your supervisor to move you on to parliamentary democracy versus republicanism. I will need some background information for my election speech."

Marcus doesn't look straight at her, but just as he is about to turn away, he slips a note under her compudule.

Colette waits for a while after he has left and then retrieves the note. It says simply: *Can we meet at the apartment the day after tomorrow? I know it's a Wednesday, a work day, but it's important. Let me know what time you will be there.*

Colette blinks back tears and tears up the note. *I'm not going to reply to him,* she vows. *I don't want to ever go to the apartment again. I'm not going to swim around that Wire and risk being electrocuted or eaten by a shark, or spotted by the authorities – just to pander to him.* All day she ruminates over the matter. She feels so hurt. Her whole world looks dark and she can't see any hope of happiness. *What a dope I was,* she thinks *and what a rat he is!*

That evening Rodney comes around to see her. He sees she is upset and tries to brighten her up.

"Some of us are going to see a special Charlie Chaplin film tonight, would you like to come?" he asks.

Colette agrees to join him. It would be better than sitting around moping.

After the film, Rodney walks her back along the beach promenade, still concerned at her depressed demeanor.

"What's wrong, Col?" he asks. "Have I said something wrong? Or is something bad happening at work?'

Colette can't tell him what is really upsetting her, instead, she tells him about the draconian regime she is about to undergo after the injections and the pills and the procedure and the resulting pregnancy.

"Wow!" Rodney exclaims. "That's truly gruesome. Would you like me to come back with you tonight? We can have a cuddle."

"No," says Colette, shaking her head. "I can't. I'm not allowed to have sex with anyone while I'm undergoing the preparation treatment in case I get pregnant."

"But isn't that what's it all for – to get pregnant?"

"Well yes, and no," Colette. replies. "I have to get pregnant to whoever the authorities have chosen as the very best genetic fit so that my baby can be as perfect as possible."

And she starts to sob again. "You'd better go now, Rodney, I'm not going to be much fun at the moment," Then she takes a deep breath, "In fact, Rodney, although I'm very fond of you, I think it's time we broke up. I think you'll have no trouble finding someone else – Melanie, for example, is secretly pining for you. I think we should just be good friends from now on."

Rodney gives her a bear hug and tries to calm her.

"I'll see you tomorrow and things might look better in the morning," he suggests.

Colette shakes her head. "No, Rodney, our arrangement is now over, but as I said, I hope we can stay very good friends."

Colette goes back to her apartment alone. As she closes her door, she brightens momentarily, at least the pregnancy regime will provide her with a legitimate reason to turn down the Elders' leader, Alistair's, invitation to act as the Elders' front woman for the election. *Any mention of pregnancy would turn them right off me,* she thinks. *The old tarts!* And she sits down and sends Alistair an email declining their 'kind offer'.

Next morning, she doesn't feel much brighter, but she forces herself to get dressed and go to the office and get stuck into her new research task. Around 11am a message flashes on her screen.

It just says: "What time tomorrow?"

Colette refuses to reply.

Just before she leaves the office for the evening, another message flashes up.

AFTER THE ULTIMATE VIRUS

"What time tomorrow? This is urgent. A cab will pick you up from the corner of the main Esplanade. You must come. This is a very serious matter"

Colette thinks carefully. No matter what she feels now about Marcus, she has to be careful. He is the Chief Administrator and her job, her whole existence, depends on his whim. She will have to obey him. So she replies "10.30am."

Next morning Colette packs a pair of casual trousers and a T-shirt into a bag, along with her swipe card for the door chain at Pacific Avenue. She feels numb. *It'll be dreadful now to see Marcus in the apartment, our secret apartment...*

She tells her supervisor she will need to go to the central data repository that morning to follow up what the Chief Administrator has asked her to research. She then sits down at her desk and busies herself until 10.15am when she leaves the building and walks down the Esplanade to the corner. At 10.30am an electric cab arrives and opens its door for her to get in. As they drive off, she quickly starts to change out of her office top and trousers into her more casual attire. *Driverless cabs do have their virtues – they don't have prying eyes!* she thinks.

Arriving at the entrance to No 2 Pacific Avenue, Colette waves to Lorf and Hazel, who wave back as she hurries through to the staircase. As she climbs the steps she notes that the second landing and stairs leading up from it had been swept clean. No fishbones anywhere. She reaches the apartment and gets out her swipe card to open the padlock, but finds it is already unlocked. Pushing open the door, she steps into the main room, to find it has also been swept clean. Standing in the middle of the room is Marcus.

"Good, Colette, I was afraid you mightn't come."

Colette mumbles something and doesn't look straight at him.

They go out onto the balcony and sit down. Colette doesn't say anything, and Marcus looks at her quizzically. "What's bugging you, Colette? You did so brilliantly at the party – and you looked so lovely. What's wrong? Have I said or done something to upset you?"

Colette can't contain herself any longer. Trying to sound cool, she begins "I saw you the other day – at the Infirmary."

"Oh?" he replies, "I didn't see you. If I'd known you would be there I'd have at least said hello."

Colette looks at him for a long moment. "Who was that dark-haired woman you were talking to?" she asks as calmly as she can.

"Oh, you mean Annie? She's my clone sister. – she was cloned from my clone-father's sister. She's the chief doctor there and she's one of my little team of supporters. I'm thinking of putting her in charge of Health for the Colony."

Colette lets out a sob of relief. Marcus looks at her in surprise. "What's the matter, Colette? You've been acting strangely the past few days?"

Tears streaming down her face, Colette finds herself laughing and crying all at once.

"No, Marcus," she almost whispers. "Everything's fine. Absolutely fine."

He leans over to her and puts his arm around her, an expression of understanding coming over his face. "Did you think Annie was another woman I was involved with? Did you?"

Colette nods dumbly.

"Colette! You're the only woman I care for. I love you dearly."

He pushes her hair out of her eyes and kisses her passionately. She feels her whole body responding, vibrating to him.

"Come on Colette, it's about time we went to bed," Marcus says, starting to lead her inside the apartment.

"But we don't have a bed," Colette interrupts him.

"Oh yes we do," he replies, opening the main bedroom door. Colette looks in and sees a large inflatable bed spread out on the floor, covered with a sumptuous oriental cover and piled with enormous cushions also covered in oriental fabric. She laughs. "Oh Marcus! You do think of everything!"

Together, they fall upon the bed. Marcus lifts off her T-shirt and trousers and takes off his top and shorts. Lying together they kiss again and start to make love. Colette feels overwhelmed by his electric touch on her breasts. She has never experienced love-making like this before and she moans in complete ecstasy as he comes to her in a climax of delicious passion.

AFTER THE ULTIMATE VIRUS

"I love you Colette. I love you," Marcus whispers in her ear. "I need to come again – now!" And they make love again.

Finally, exhausted and overwhelmed by it all, they lie together on the oriental cover and laugh.

"That was something else again!" Colette exclaims, "I... love you too, Marcus. That's the first time I have ever said that to anyone."

Marcus turns over and looks deeply into her eyes. "You and I have a lot of unfinished business to complete," he says cryptically, "And much more new business to do. Let's have a quick brunch and I'll tell you more about what's been happening. And maybe we might find time to make a return trip to our bedroom before we have to go."

They sit side-by-side on the balcony, with Marcus's arm around her shoulders, "We're going to have to be very careful nobody sees us together – at least until the election," Marcus says. "I'm doing something very illegal, transgressing the Colony's Rule that managers must not enter into relationships with their staff. But I couldn't wait any longer to be with you. The Elders have their spies everywhere, so we'll have to be ultra-careful."

As before, he has brought some delicious snacks: Smoked salmon and caviar, oysters, and more of his exquisite fried rice. Where on earth did he get rice from? Colette wonders. After the feast she'd enjoyed at Karla's, she is beginning to suspect that there's a special farm somewhere secret, producing these rare delicacies. Once again, Marcus has brought some wine, white this time. "This white wine's not going to last much longer," he laments. "It's very, very old. We must start growing our own grapes. I believe there's quite good wine-growing soil out west towards the Mountains – the old colonists grew grapes there."

Then he looks serious. "The Elders are pulling out all the stops to beat me, and a lot has been happening over the past couple of days," he begins. "Now that we know, thanks to you, the date of the election, we've been getting organised. Suyen has drawn up a schedule and has been designing posters and flyers, and we've checked with the TV station to make sure we have plenty of slots booked. I now need your input about what we need to say to get our message over.

ALARUMS AND EXCURSIONS

"At the moment, as you know from the meeting down at my place last week, we're planning to stand on a platform of reform and improvement of life in the Colony: Time for Change, as they used to say back in the Olden Days.

"You know how we want to open up the housing availability, start a marketplace, encourage farming

"And we want to put a clean broom through the bureaucracy which is presently stifling enterprise and creativity.

"We will also present a glimpse of greater things to come: building a new nation, expanding the electricity grid, starting manufacturing, etc. But we don't want to frighten the Colony with too many grand ideas. People don't like change. We need to pace our reforms. And first of all, we need to win the election.

"I've co-opted Rodney into the Gully Group and he's keen to improve the sporting facilities, and we're going to promote this. And we're planning to hold the Colony's first surf carnival next Sunday where I will be introduced as the carnival organiser and I'll grab an opportunity to outline our campaign."

Colette agrees with all Marcus says, but she wants him to add something she feels strongly about: the pregnancy regime and how the women in the Colony have to suffer the brunt of this program, losing precious years of job advancement, and, after going through two pregnancies, not being allowed any meaningful contact with their babies.

Marcus listens intently to what she is saying.

"I'd never really thought much about this," he confesses. "It has been so much an integral part of our life in the Colony – and being a man, it didn't impinge too much on me – apart from having to be a sperm donor from time-to-time. But now you point out its iniquities, I realise we must make it an important part of our election platform.

"We must promise to reward every woman who undergoes, or has undergone in the past, the pregnancy program. What do you suggest would be a fair reward?"

Colette thinks for a moment and then says: "I think, for a start, that each time a woman has gone through the program, she should be promoted one year in her Level in the administration bureaucracy. That's the least that could be done, but it would be a start. And I suggest that the Nannies be included in this plan. They

71

are selfless women who do the hard slog in bringing up each generation of clones and now the progeny of the artificially inseminated mothers. I love my Nanny, she was kind and taught me so much! They deserve some reward too."

"It's a deal, Colette," exclaims Marcus. "Women make up 50 percent of the Colony's population, this is likely to bring us 50 percent of the vote!"

"Yes," agrees Colette. "It has been the elephant in the room for a very long time."

"Can I leave you to get this message out, Colette?" Marcus asks. "You have a wide network of women friends."

"Yes," Colette replies. "I certainly will. Leave this to me – and don't query any of my tactics!"

Marcus promises, and gives her a big kiss.

"Now," he says, starting to gather up the plates and glasses. "I'd like to get some work done here on the apartment to make it more livable. I'll get Charlie to bring a couple of his Army mates over next Saturday to sort out the solar panels on the roof and to clean out the water tank and get the plumbing working. I'll see if they might be able to get some water down to the tap in the garage for Lorf's crowd too. And I need help in de-rusting the fridge. I hope you agree with this plan? So while this work is going on, would you like to come over to my place next Saturday and we can have a bush picnic in the gully?"

"Of course, that sounds lovely. I've never been in the bush before," Colette says. Then she adds: "You'd better explain to Lorf what's going to happen up on the roof here."

Marcus agrees he would.

And they go inside and back into the bedroom.

12

DON'T ROCK THE BOAT

COLETTE WAKES up next morning feeling ecstatically happy. Marcus is the first man she's ever met who made her feel that way.

The possibility of an illicit pregnancy flashes through her mind briefly. *To hell with that,* she thinks, dismissing the idea – like so many other women have over the ages. *I'm just so happy.* Anyway, unless she refuses to have anything further to do with Marcus – and that's totally out of the question – she'd have to take the risk. After all, in the Colony male contraceptives don't exist, because all the girls are inoculated against pregnancy and remain unable to conceive until they are put through the pregnancy program.– she'll simply have to bear the consequences is she does get pregnant by Marcus.

That day, Colette goes on with her research, a happy feeling rising in her mind whenever she thinks of Marcus. In the evening, she goes back to her apartment and takes out the folder of material about her clone mother, Sophie, which she had removed from the filing cabinet at Pacific Avenue. It is about time she had another look at the material she has salvaged. She feels her hands trembling as she unties a dark red ribbon that is tied around the folder. *It obviously contains something precious, for it to be tied up with a ribbon.* Turning over the folder's cover, she finds an envelope containing a disc. Would it fit into her module? To her delight, the disc does fit, and she's able to activate it. What would she find on it? Colette stands up and checks her hatch to see if her dinner has arrived. There it is, still hot, so she takes it out and places it on her desk next to her portable module Taking a quick bite of her meal, she turns her concentration back to the disc. It contains three files of photographs. The first is titled "Business Trips, Asia and Europe". The second is titled "Family and

73

Friends." The third: "Jim and Me". Colette homes in straight away to the third file, asking her module to open it. The disc contains 3D photos, not holographs, for which she's thankful. Holographs might not have worked on her module. She clicks on the first photo and sees a picture of herself. Blue eyes, blondish-red hair, a mole above her right cheekbone. But of course, it isn't her, it was Sophie, her clone-mother. Sophie was standing in front of an enormous rocket plane. She was carrying a suitcase and was obviously about to set off on a flight to somewhere. Had Jim taken the shot? Would there be photos of Jim? Colette turns back anxiously to the disc and clicks on a second file. It's another picture of Sophie, this time running along the beach in a bikini, laughing in the sun. The third file is yet another photo of Sophie, dressed very elegantly in evening clothes, sitting at a table lit by candles, leaning forward to speak to someone who must have been sitting on the other side of the table. *Was that Jim?* Colette begins to fear she'll never get a glimpse of Jim – he was obviously taking all the pictures. Then she asks her module to open the next one. What she sees leaves her stunned. It is a photograph of Marcus holding Sophie's hand! *But what was Marcus doing there? How could he have been there? Those photos had been taken 70 years ago!* But it *is* Marcus, the same black hair, the same determined chin, the same hazel-brown eyes, the same quick smile – and the same sexy-looking legs.

The truth hits Colette like a knife. Marcus is Jim's clone. Jim was Marcus's clone-father! Is this just a weird coincidence? Or is it Fate? Colette is dumbfounded. She sits leaning her chin on her hands, toying with her evening meal, wondering about her discovery and gradually starting to think how this might affect her still very tenuous relationship with Marcus. *We hardly know each other yet. Maybe Marcus would be embarrassed by the knowledge. Maybe he would be intimidated by the thought of history repeating itself?* She already feels self-conscious herself about the discovery, knowing how close

DON'T ROCK THE BOAT

Sophie and Jim had been. Indeed, they had been married for many, many years. Maybe Marcus would shy away from her, not wanting to repeat history? Colette decides to go up to the roof garden on top of her building and get some fresh air. The cool evening breeze calms her. The clear night sky displays its canopy of stars, and down below, the waves heave and roll. Colette looks out over the Colony and makes a decision: She would not tell Marcus what she has discovered – at least for the moment. She would conceal the disc and put it back in her wardrobe, showing Marcus only the photos of Sophie at work on assignment. She simply doesn't want to rock the boat.

Over the next days the election campaign is announced and becomes quite vicious. The Elders have mobilised a large number of people who have received favours over the years and who are thus indebted to them. Their campaign centres on Marcus being a traitor to the Colony. "This traitor will destroy the Colony and take us back to the terrors of The Calamity" is their message – and it resonates with many of the residents in the Colony, particularly the older ones. For them, life had settled into a predictable pattern. They had sufficient food, and they could go up the Mall for entertainment. The Elders put their message across skilfully on TV and through their posters.

Even more insidious is the action taken against Marcus by certain senior members of the bureaucracy staff who start counteracting orders he has made. This disruption to the usual smooth running of the Colony's services makes people uncertain about voting for Marcus. The supervisor of garbage removal, for instance, who is in Montgomery's pocket, disobeys Marcus' order to double the service on Sunday evenings after the weekly barbecues down the beach. A lot of people complain about the mess. Marcus is supposed to be in charge, isn't he?

Marcus and the Gully Group are being painted and smeared as "dangerous radicals" and the Elders are predicting the election will be a walkover for them.

Colette is worried. It would be a tragedy if the Elders were to win, and she wracks her brain in search of a way to counteract the Elders' evil propaganda. The phrase 'the elephant in the room' keeps jangling in her mind, and suddenly she comes up with a daring and possibly crazy idea. On her Monday lunch break she goes to see Phil where he is having a sandwich at his desk in the Department of Housing.

"Phil," Colette begins. "I've been given a specific issue to promote in the run-up to the election, and Marcus has given me carte blanche to do whatever I think will help our cause."

"Of course, I'm only too happy to help," Phil says. "But what is it that you want me to do?"

"I need an empty water tank," Colette says with a winsome smile. "Could you lend me one for a couple of weeks?"

Somewhat puzzled, Phil agrees to her request. "But what's it for?" he asks.

"That must remain a secret for the moment," Colette replies. "And I'm very grateful. Could you please have the tank delivered to the old gym down the road from the beach?"

Then Colette goes over to the Army HQ and asks to see Charlie. Beaming, he comes to the front desk and asks what she wants.

Explaining she's planning something for the election, she tells Charlie: "I need a small truck, big enough to carry a water tank lying on its side. I'll need a dual electric-manual truck because it will need to start and stop at odd intervals. Can you help?"

Like Phil, Charlie is puzzled, but he's fond of Colette and knows she's no fool. So he happily agrees to help.

"Anything you need, Colette, is at your disposal," he promises.

"Thanks, Charlie," Colette replies. "Would you be able to deliver it into the yard at the back of the old gym and get someone to help load a water tank onto the back of the truck?"

Next, Colette goes over to the Nannies' retirement boarding house and asks to see her old Nanny who is now about 88.

"Nanny," Colette says, "I need your help." She explains the secret of her mission to her because her Nanny knows her so well and wouldn't be brushed off by prevarication. "So I need you and your fellow Nannies to do a lot of important sewing for me," Colette says.

DON'T ROCK THE BOAT

"It's in a very good cause – and about time!" the old woman replies with a laugh.

Finally, Colette pays a visit to the central depot and puts in a request for 100 metres of grey felt – underfelt used for putting under carpets. The depot supervisor looks suspiciously at Colette, who pacifies him by explaining it is to be used at an election rally, and could it please be delivered to the old gym?

Colette's last task is to ask Rodney whether he could be available to drive a truck during the final week of the campaign. Like the others, Rodney is puzzled at her request, but he agrees to help.

While she is having a late lunch, Colette goes to Melanie and her workmates and asks them if they'd like to help her in a secret election project down at the gym – after work – each evening. Intrigued, they happily agree to meet her that evening at the gym.

Colette then returns to her office and gets on with her work. Each evening she goes to the gym to supervise her secret project and by the end of the week it's almost ready. She receives a note from Marcus on the Friday, saying just: *Cab will pick you up usual place 10am Saturday,* and when she gets home she rummages in her wardrobe and finds an old pair of shorts suitable for a bush picnic.

Then off to the old gym to continue supervising her secret project.

13

THE WATERHOLE

COLETTE ARRIVES at Marcus's yellow house at 10.20am. It is the first time she has visited it in the daytime. It's a glorious late spring day, not a cloud in the sky, and there is a hazy, lazy pre-summery feel about it. Marcus is waiting on the veranda and they go into the kitchen to sort out the picnic things. Colette observes that his kitchen is simple but well-organised, with shelves neatly stacked with jars of all shapes and contents. There's a scrubbed wooden table and an old fridge that had probably belonged to whoever had owned the house way back in the Olden Days. The kitchen bears all the signs of belonging to a committed cook.

"Here's a basket of food for you to carry, my darling," Marcus says, pausing to give Colette a kiss. "And I'll take the drinks, the rug and the beach umbrella, and some hats to fend off this surprisingly hot sun."

As they leave the Gully House, Colette looks back at it. "I love its yellow colour," she says, "But how come you chose yellow?"

"Well," replies Marcus. "I found the Gully House quite a long time ago, when I was still in the middle ranks of the bureaucracy. I came across the house one day when I was on a surveying assignment of the nearby beaches and managed to get a permanent pass through the Wire, so I decided to live in the house. It needed a new coat of paint, but the only colour of paint available to me on my ranking was yellow. I guess that was because yellow was the colour least in demand. So I painted my house yellow. But I like the colour too."

"So you painted the house by yourself?" asks Colette.

"Yes, I liked being out in the fresh air and sun and I enjoyed the exercise and seeing the house transformed," he replies.

THE WATERHOLE

Then they set off, walking down the road towards the beach, turning off onto a dirt track leading into dense bushland. Currawongs call high above them, and Colette can hear chirpings and buzzings coming from the low scrub. She can see bright red bush flowers and recognises waratahs from her evening at Karla's where there had been waratahs in the fireplace. A bird cackles from a tall gum tree, and she realises it must be a laughing kookaburra. A little lizard scuttles across the track. This is all new to Colette; she has never been in the bush before – there is no bushland in the inner Colony inside the Wire.

"We'll walk a little way along this track," says Marcus, "and then we'll go down to the pond – or it should be called a waterhole, I guess. It's a lovely spot for a picnic – it'll be good to relax for a while. This election campaign is starting to get very busy. I have to see so many people all over the Colony, and up-and-down the coast as well. I'm very grateful to you for all the work you're doing, not only preparing material for my speeches, but spreading the message about our campaign platform, especially about the rewards for women."

"I've certainly been spreading the word," Colette replies, "and I've now got the Nannies on side. They, too, are spreading the word. Your message is starting to get through. But I must admit, there's a lot of anti-Marcus propaganda being spread around too. The Elders are very vicious about you."

"Yes," concedes Marcus. "The odds are against us winning, but our Gully Group is gaining members by the day. We have youthful enthusiasm on our side, even if we lack the sophisticated campaign methods of the Elders. Everyone is trying their hardest and it's great to see their enthusiasm. It gives me hope yet for the Colony."

They reach a fork in the track and Marcus leads Colette down the left-hand one. "This is the way to the pond – the waterhole."

Soon they can hear the sound of a little waterfall tumbling down a low cliff and then Colette peers through the trees and spots a shady glade with a rock pool, its clear water glinting in the shafts of sunlight filtering through the trees.

"What a lovely place for a picnic!" she exclaims.

"Yes," says Marcus, spreading the blanket out under a tree close to the side of the pond. We'll put the umbrella up, too, but it's quite shady and out of the hot sun here."

They set up the picnic food and Marcus opens the container of ice and drinks. "It's a bit too early for wine. How about a soft drink?"

Colette stretches out on the rug and shakes her sandals off. She feels in something of a daze. The new bushland sights and sounds fascinate her, and she turns to Marcus, who has lain down on the rug beside her,

"Marcus, I'm so happy," she says. "These last few weeks have been the happiest in my life."

Marcus leans over and kisses her. "Yes," he replies. "I'm very, very happy too. Thank god I've found you."

Colette suddenly feels that this is the moment to divulge what she has found out about Jim being Marcus's clone-father, a matter which she hadn't wanted to mention yet, for fear that it might spoil everything. But suddenly, she feels it is time to mention it.

"Marcus," she begins, and hesitates.

"Yes?" he inquires.

"There's something I ought to tell you..."

"Oh?" asks Marcus.

"When I was going through my clone-mother, Sophie's folders from the filing cabinet in the apartment at Pacific Avenue, I came across some interesting photos of Jim."

"Yesss," says Marcus slowly. "And why did you find them interesting?"

"Well," says Colette, hesitatingly. "They are the spitting image of you!" She looks at Marcus tentatively.

"Yes!" Marcus laughs. "I know. Jim was my clone-father. I've known it all along, but I didn't know the link to Sophie for ages, and more lately, the link to you. I didn't want to mention it to you until I was sure that everything between us was fine. I didn't want to impose on you a relationship that had been so strong in the past in case it might frighten you – or put you off me. I didn't want to rock the boat."

Colette is open-mouthed. "So you knew all along!" she exclaims. "And I didn't want to tell **you** because *I* didn't want to rock the boat either." And she leans over and gives Marcus a hug.

THE WATERHOLE

"Yes," he goes on. "When I first set eyes on you two years ago, I was immediately attracted to you. I was determined to find out all about you. I hadn't found anyone after Karla who remotely interested me, and then, when I saw you – you were down in the canteen with a group of your friends – I knew I had to get to know you. So I did some research and found out more about you, including who your clone-mother was, and the records showed that Sophie was married to my clone-father, Jim.

"I didn't do anything about this for quite a while. I didn't want to tempt fate. I knew that both of us had grown up in very different circumstances to that of Jim and Sophie. I wanted to observe you for a while. I read a lot of what you'd culled from your Big Data research and I realised I was dealing with someone intelligent, but I still wanted to see if you had that special spark in you that I craved. And I didn't want to interfere in your life if you had already found someone you cared for deeply."

Colette laughs: "And then you finally called me into your office and I rebelled against you when you forbade me from searching for my clone-mother's details!"

"And thank god, you did rebel," concludes Marcus. "Now let's go down to the pond and have a swim before lunch."

"But I haven't brought my bathers," Colette protests.

"Who needs bathers?" asks Marcus, already stripping off his T-shirt and undoing the belt buckle on his shorts.

Colette strips off her clothes too, and the two of them step down on to the rocks beside the pond, peering into the clear water to see, reflected, their naked bodies forming and reforming in circular ripples across the surface of the pond.

"Come on in!" calls Marcus, striding into the water. "It's lovely and cool."

Colette follows him and plunges in, swimming across to the other side of the pond and then diving under the water. They duck and dive like two playful otters until they meet up on the other side of the pond where some reeds are growing. Marcus watches Colette's body curving and shimmering in the water, and dives down, coming up and standing in the shallower water beside her. He puts his arms around her and draws her back into the deeper water where they stand together, their heads just above the surface. They embrace and kiss, and Marcus runs his hands over her breasts and down her body as they stand there in the deep water. He grasps her slippery buttocks and pulls her closer.

"Come…Marcus…come!" she cries, thrusting herself towards him. And they come together in an underwater orgasm that shakes them both.

Laughing, they stagger together to the other side of the pond and climb out, flopping onto the towels Marcus has brought.

"That was out of this world!" he exclaims.

"I've never had sex underwater before," Colette says, towelling her bedraggled hair.

"Nor have I," Marcus confesses.

"At one stage I thought I might drown," Colette says.

"You shouldn't have worried – I'd have administered mouth-to-mouth resuscitation," Marcus replies.

"Oh, is that what you were doing?" asks Colette.

"It was absolutely superb, but I think I prefer the comfort of a bed," Marcus says.

"Yes," Colette agree. "It was totally brilliant, but a bed is dryer."

They get up and walk back up to the picnic basket, pull on their discarded clothes and sit down on the rug, enjoying its warmth.

Marcus lays out some plates and opens up a container of cold chicken and fish and lettuce, and stuffed curried eggs with mint. He butters some brown bread rolls and cuts up some tomatoes and cloves of garlic.

"This is a simple repast. No caviar today," he says.

Suddenly the cicadas begin to throb, louder and louder, until they reach a screeching continuous crescendo. Marcus pours some wine and they recline under the umbrella.

"Marcus," Colette says drowsily, "what did you learn about Jim?"

"Not a great deal," Marcus replies. "In fact, I learned more about him after you found Sophie's diary. But I did know that his father was an engineer, building bridges, and Jim was a celebrated journalist. I found some articles he wrote in the Olden Days, but I couldn't find much of his later TV or radio stuff in The Best of Times because most of that went out live and they didn't store it.

"But I did find that he was a valued employee of old Sir Milton West, the multi-billionaire media tycoon who was the third generation of West Media tycoons. Old West used to live in that house of Karla's you visited for the party."

"Would Sophie have been employed by West too?" Colette inquires.

"Yes, indeed, she was. They would have gone to parties at Christmas time at that house."

"So...," Colette says, "maybe that's why I felt I'd been in that house before. Remember how I told you that the rear of the house had a large laundry and then a kitchen? I kept on feeling this eerie sensation that I'd been there before."

Marcus looks at her. "Well, maybe Sophie's DNA somehow absorbed her impressions of the house and somehow this stayed in her DNA and was passed on to you. But I have never experienced that feeling of *déjà vu* about the house, yet Jim would have been there many times. Maybe our different DNAs select different impressions. It's a very interesting matter and we should look into this phenomenon more."

Colette rolls over and picks a long stem of grass and chews its end. "You know, although I'm a clone I feel completely myself. I don't feel I'm someone else, do you? I'm me."

"No," replies Marcus. "I believe we clones are complete individuals – just like anyone else who is born of two parents. We all inherit DNA from our parents, whether we are born of two parents or are cloned from one. We behave partly because of our genes and partly we respond and react to the environment we are born into. Our environment is similar in some ways to what Sophie and Jim were born into, but very different in others. So naturally, we react to our environment differently, and so we're different from Sophie and Jim in certain ways."

"Mmm," Colette says, "And I guess if we were cloned somewhere else – say Mars – we'd adapt ourselves to that environment and be different from what we are here."

"Yes," Marcus replies, "I agree, but now I'm going to have a snooze."

They doze on together until the afternoon shadows begin to filter across the clearing and it's time to go. Tomorrow is the Surf Carnival and they both would have a busy day.

AFTER THE ULTIMATE VIRUS

That evening, lying in her hammock back at her apartment, Colette thinks about Marcus. Their relationship has deepened in the past few days, and she's beginning to find a lot more about him. He is definitely strong-minded, and extremely capable – he couldn't have reached the top of the bureaucracy without being tough, clever, and crafty. But there is much more that she is just starting to sense about him. He has a quiet certainty about him, as if he were pursuing a private agenda that can't be ruffled or upset by the antics or opinions of people around him. He possesses, too, the ability to lead people, to inspire them to do their best, and his calm assurance impresses her. But he is also sensitive to others' feelings, she now knew. His mind is quick and powerful and unconventional, and she's enjoying stretching her own mid to meet his. For her whole life until now, she realises, she had been operating at half-capacity. Marcus stimulates her to think…and of course, he is physically overwhelmingly attractive. *I'm going to have great fun getting to know him better*…she thinks dreamily as she dozes off.

14

CAUGHT IN THE RIP

THERE ISN'T a cloud in the sky on Sunday morning, and by 7am the spectator seats for the Surf Carnival have been erected and the beach volleyball nets set up for the competitions. A striped umbrella over a hamburger stall is placed under a Norfolk Island pine, and two ancient wooden surf boats, which Rodney's team have uncovered in a dilapidated boat shed along the point, are pulled up high on the sand, ready for their races.

Colette has brought an old pair of binoculars she had found in the junk warehouse, and she wanders around, looking for Marcus and Rodney and the rest of the Gully Group who are organising the first surf carnival the Colony has ever had. Soon the smell of frying onions and hamburgers fills the air, ready for early morning breakfasters. Rodney is rushing about, fixing the sound system, starting up the music, checking that the repairs to the surf boats has been completed, and erecting flags on the sand to indicate where people could swim and where the races would be staged.

Marcus arrives and comes towards her. Colette notices he's wearing shorts and a Hawaiian-style shirt.

"The girls will go for those legs of yours," she laughs, greeting him. To her surprise, Marcus blushes.

"Well, I hope they hold up in the beach volleyball comp...my legs, I mean."

They wander together down to the beachfront and then go their separate ways, aware that the prying eyes of the Elders' supporters would report all they saw.

Finally, at 10am, the carnival is ready to begin, hundreds of Colonists have been streaming in, bringing towels and rugs and hats and sunglasses, ready for the big day. Soon, more than a thousand have arrived, and more are coming along the Esplanade.

Many of them have never heard of a Surf Carnival. Others know vaguely that they had been especially big in the Olden Days, back in the 1950s, before motorised rubber duckies had been introduced. All are amazed when they see the line of surf lifesavers, the males wearing brief bathing togs (once called "budgie smugglers") and the girls in bikinis, all wearing striped cotton caps, lined up, carrying enormous flags. They drill professionally up-and-down the beach; Rodney has outdone himself with the organisation.

Then the music is turned up with a roll of drums and Marcus strides on to the platform in front of the seats and greets the crowd through a microphone the techos have wired up.

Colette, sitting in the stands, hears people around her, mainly girls, murmuring when they see Marcus.

"So that's what the Chief Administrator looks like!" one of the girls remarks. "He doesn't look like an evil ogre like those posters say he is."

Another girl adds: "He looks quite cool to me. Like his style."

'Cool', muses Colette. *That's old slang from the late 20th century. She must have picked it up from an old movie she's seen.*

Marcus steps up to the platform and welcomes everyone, explaining what is to take place. There would be swimming races in the surf, alternating with beach volleyball contests on the sand until noon. Then there would be displays of life-saving with old-fashioned surf-reels and, later, after lunch, the big contests between the two surf boat crews.

"And with this surf looking like it's going to rise as the day goes on, the surf boat comp should be worth watching," he promises.

He goes on to give a brief list of what the Colony could expect if he won the election and finishes by saying "We hope that if we win the election we'll hold plenty more surf carnivals! They're part of our plan to liven up the Colony!"

Then Rodney gets up with a megaphone and shouts: "Vote Marcus for more surf fun!"

A supporter in the crowd shouts back: "Good on yer, Marcus!" Everybody clap and cheer, and the Carnival contests begin. Colette has heard a few hisses from Elders' supporters, but they are nothing compared to the cheers from the rest of the crowd. *There's hope yet,* she prays.

Sitting in the stands, Colette watches the swimming races with groups of boys, and then men, battling through the breakers to reach a row of buoys in the blue water outside the white foam, and then swimming back to shore again.

Then came the beach volleyball championships: all-male, all-female, and mixed. She is interested to see Marcus taking part in the all-male contest, playing powerfully and helping to score vital goals.

The girls sitting behind her are impressed. "He doesn't just have nice legs." one comments. "He's a pretty good player."

Colette is pleased. This surf carnival would do a lot of good for Marcus's image.

Next, the lifesavers put on a display of marching, and then they stage a mock rescue using an old-style rope reel which they measure out into the surf over their heads.

By now the sun is high in the sky and the temperature has risen to the mid-30s, unseasonably high for late spring It is time for lunch, and the barbecues are sizzling. Colette has never seen so many people at the beach, and she spots Marcus being mobbed by people eager to find out more about the election, and to tell him what they think should be done with the Colony. She doesn't notice many of the Elders there. Obviously, surf carnivals are not to their refined taste.

After lunch, the major event of the carnival begins: a series of daring onslaughts into the ever-stronger waves by two teams of lifesavers rowing the two ancient wooden surf boats which lurch high up the walls of waves and then down the other side as the rollers break, rushing into the shore.

Colette looks up at the sky and sees thunder clouds forming in the South-West. The wind is rising too, and the waves battling the surf boats are crashing down onto the shore like thunder. Colette picks up her binoculars to see if she can find Marcus, but she can't see him anywhere. Finally, she spots him wandering alone along the shore, obviously needing a break from the crowd. As she watches him, she suddenly sees a young girl who has somehow escaped her Nanny's care, being swept out to sea by the waves a long way down the beach where it is known to be a dangerous part of the suf. The girl doesn't look more than ten and she's struggling and screaming.

Colette sees Marcus spot the girl and dive into the surf towards her. The waves down that end of the beach are enormous and there is a dangerous area there called The Rip which drags a current from the shore out to sea.

Oh my god, Colette thinks, getting up from her seat and making her way down to the ground. She starts running along the Esplanade towards Marcus and the girl. She can see he has reached the girl and is holding her against his chest while he fights the waves. Slowly, he manages to turn the girl around and begins dragging her towards the shore. But The Rip is starting to get the better of him.

Colette feels totally helpless as she watches Marcus. She takes her phone out of her pocket and rings Rodney, but he doesn't answer.

Then she tries the local police station. A lone voice answers and she explains what is happening. The duty policeman says he'll call the ambulance immediately and would contact the remainder of the Colony's three-man police force, who are attending the Carnival.

Having done that, Colette then rings the Colony TV station. "The Chief Administrator is battling the surf to save a young girl, from drowning. They are both in danger of drowning!" she tells them. "Can you divert your cameraman to the south end of the beach??"

Meanwhile, Marcus struggles to reach the shore. Thunder rolls out of the clouds and zigzags of lightning shoot down into the sea which has turned an uneasy, green-yellow colour.

This is a scene from hell! Colette thinks as she runs from the Esplanade across the sand to the water's edge. "Marcus!" she shouts, "Marcus, keep going!"

Soon a small crowd of people gather to watch. One of the surf boats has been alerted and has turned to row down towards the struggling Marcus. *Would they get there in time to help him?* Colette writhes with anguish.

Then an extra-large wave comes in, throwing Marcus and the girl up high and then dumping them forward. Marcus takes this opportunity to lunge forward, and his feet touch the sand. As the retreating wave sucks him back, he makes one last stride, pulling the girl by her arms up the sloping sand to the shore.

The ambulance men have arrived and take out a stretcher, laying the girl on it and checking her to gauge how much water she has swallowed. She starts coughing up water – she's alive. Then they turn to Marcus, who is sitting on the sand, exhausted.

"Well done, sir," says one of the ambulancemen, "Are you injured? Can we check your blood pressure?"

Colette rushes up and puts her hands on Marcus's shoulders, "Marcus, my darling! Thank god you survived!"

Marcus gives her a little smile and tries to say something, but he's out of breath.

Then the TV crew come up and start filming him and Colette carefully withdraws into the crowd.

"Mr Administrator, congratulations on a very brave effort," says the TV interviewer. "We managed to catch the last part of your rescue. You were very courageous."

"Well," Marcus says humbly. "I just happened to be in the right place at the right time."

"But obviously you are a good swimmer," says the TV man. "Do you surf often?"

"Yes," Marcus replies. "I try to take a surf every morning before work."

Somebody comes and wraps a towel around him and someone else brings him a cup of tea.

Marcus thanks them and then gets up, saying:

"There's going to be a big storm. We'd all better make a break for it before we get struck by lightning!"

And with that, he turns back to Colette and says: "I think I've done my dash for the day – in fact, I'm buggered. I've got a cab waiting for me to take me home. I'd dearly love to take you with me but we can't be seen together in public – yet.

"Can you come to my house tomorrow evening for a meeting with the Gully Group? I'll book your cab to come a bit earlier than the others', so we can see each other."

Colette blows him a surreptitious little kiss and nods agreement.

"See you tomorrow," she says.

15

THE ELEPHANT IN THE ROOM

THE COLONY is abuzz next day with Marcus's surf rescue. Everybody has seen it on TV and are impressed, but then the Elders start a smear campaign on TV and via mobile phones, alleging the whole rescue was nothing but a publicity stunt devised by Marcus and his team to attract favourable publicity.

That evening, when she arrives at Marcus's yellow house, Colette asks him what they could do to counteract the slurs of the Elders.

"Nothing," he replies. "to respond would be to elevate their slurs to a level of importance they don't warrant. It's best if we simply disregard them."

"Well I'm going to tell everyone I know the truth," Colette says.

"Go to it, girl," replies Marcus, squeezing her hand. "The more counter-propaganda you can generate by word-of-mouth, the better."

They are sitting arm-in-arm on the veranda sofa, waiting for the rest of the Gully Group to arrive. The election is just over six weeks away, and things are starting to get very nasty. They have serious tactics to discuss

The meeting gets underway as soon as the others arrive. Marcus outlines their next moves, explaining that the following weekend, he and Suyen and Simon would drive down to the South Coast to rally the support of the relatively small, but nonetheless important. number, of inhabitants of several tiny towns and the larger former city there.

"We'll address the need to boost farming down there. Simon's an expert on agriculture and he will get on well with the farmers. It used to be particularly good dairy territory and the locals can revive that fairly easily – there are still enough cows – and bulls – around, wild as they are now.

"We're also going to stress the need for regional representatives in our future parliament."

The big event prior to the election, he explains, is the televised debate between the leader of the Elders, Alistair, or possibly his deputy, Marmeduke, on the Thursday night before the Friday election.

"I'm tipping it will be Marmeduke – he's a really nasty piece of work, the Goebbels of that group," Marcus says. "Alistair is the clever one, he keeps his mouth shut but he's the brains behind the Elders."

"Yes," agrees Colette. "Marmeduke has poor taste in art – and at Karla's party he kept spitting in my eye when he talked."

After further discussion of practical matters, Marcus calls a halt and rings for everyone's cabs, except for Colette.

"I think you two can go together in the one cab tonight," says Marcus to William and Charlie.

"I need to discuss my Friday night speech with Colette for a few minutes," he explains.

The others exchange knowing looks, and go out on to the veranda to wait for their cab, which soon arrives.

'Now we have the place to ourselves," laughs Marcus, hugging Colette "I know I should ask you to come up and see my etchings – but I don't have any. But would you like to come upstairs anyway?"

Colette smiles, and they go up to Marcus's bedroom. Her first impression of the room is how tidy and peaceful it is. A few beautiful oil paintings, no doubt gleaned from the Art Gallery in the old city, hang on the walls, and a sumptuous oriental rug is spread across the bare floorboards. Then she freezes. On the bedside table is a small revolver. Colette has never seen a real gun – the Colony doesn't run to them. Only the Colony's tiny police force has guns, and, as far as she knows, they have never found cause to use them. She goes out on to the little balcony leading from the bedroom at the back of the house and leans on the railing to recover from the surprise. *I guess he needs a gun. Living alone outside the Wire*, she thinks. It is so silent, apart from the occasional chirping of a cricket, it is hard to imagine thieves or brigands invading. She can just make out the silhouettes of trees sloping down to the ocean.

The bed is very large, and very comfortable, Colette discovers when she comes back into the bedroom and Marcus pulls her down onto it.

"Last time it was a pond, this time it's a bed!" laughs Colette. "I think I'll plump for the bed." They begin to make love gently and slowly, savouring the luxury of being together in the night.

"This is the first time we've made love in the night-time," Marcus says. "And I hope we'll be spending many, many nights together soon – entire nights, not just snatched ones. If we win the election, all will go smoothly. I'll be able to do whatever I like, and what I like is being with you.

"Of course," he adds, in a strained tone, "if we lose the election, which is fairly likely, I will be banished to a far-flung outpost in the bush."

"In which case," Colette replies, "I'd come and find you. But now I have to go."

"Yes, alas, Cinderella has to return to her lonely hammock," says Marcus, getting up and dialling a cab.

"Please tell it to drop me off at the disused gym," Colette asks as she gets dressed, "I'm involved in an after-hours project there, so my late return won't be noticed.

"Why do you keep a gun?" she adds.

"There are still armed gangs roaming about outside the Wire, he replies. "Living here alone, I'm a sitting duck."

Marcus gives her one last kiss before she steps into her cab.

"We shan't see one another until next week," he says. "I'm off to the South Coast on Wednesday and I won't be back till Tuesday. Take care, my darling."

The following days leading up to the weekend are busy for Colette who is making preparations for the debut of her Big Secret. *I'm sorry Marcus won't be here to see the Surprise,* she thinks. *But maybe that's a good thing. It might be a total flop.*

***

Sunday dawns, bright and sunny – yet again – and Colette has a very early breakfast before setting off for the old gym. Rodney and Melanie are already there.

"Let's get everyone ready," Colette says, "And off we go with our Big Surprise!"

The Sunday morning crowd down on the Esplanade and in the park beside the beach is surprised to hear a roll of drums and a trumpet fanfare coming from the other end of the Esplanade. Alerted to the sounds, everyone gathers along the footpath to see what's going on. Then around the corner comes a bizarre apparition. It is a large grey elephant, and sitting atop it is a group of women, some of them young girls, others older, and some are pregnant. Sitting on the elephant's head is Colette, dressed in a gold tunic she's found in the warehouse, and playing the trumpet. All the women are holding up placards saying:

THE ELEPHANT IN THE ROOM IS THE PREGNANCY PROGRAM...GIVE WOMEN A FAIR GO...REWARDS FOR PREGNANCY...GIVE THE COLONY'S WOMEN A REWARD – VOTE MARCUS... WE HAVE GIVEN TO THE COLONY...NOW IT'S TIME FOR A REWARD...VOTE MARCUS – REWARD WOMEN

On closer inspection of this bizarre spectacle, the puzzled crowd sees that the elephant has been constructed from a disused water tank covered with grey underfelt. Its ears and legs and trunk have been cut out of the underfelt and stuffed and sewn into shape, and its tusks have been made from the arms of an old white plastic chair. The whole beast is sitting on a truck driven by Rodney, who is having trouble seeing through the windscreen because the elephant's trunk hangs over it. After more drumming and trumpeting, the elephant stops at the entrance to the beach park where the TV crew is waiting, and Colette stands up and starts speaking through a megaphone.

"The sacrifice the women of this Colony have made, and are still making, to increase the population and save the human race has gone unthanked for far too long." she announces "It is the elephant in the room.

"Nobody dares mention it, but it affects all the women in the Colony. It sets them back a year on their work ladder and they suffer all the discomfort of pregnancy without even the reward of a baby they can keep.

"It's time the women of the Colony are rewarded for their sacrifice.

"Vote for Marcus and he will reward the women of the Colony for their selfless sacrifice!"

Someone in the crowd lets out a loud cheer and then the whole crowd claps and cheers.

"VOTE FOR MARCUS, GIVE THE WOMEN A FAIR GO!" shouts Rodney from the van window.

And with that, Colette blows her trumpet one last time. The crowd cheers and the elephant trundles back down the Esplanade, followed by young children wanting to touch it.

"How did we go?" she asks Rodney as they reach the old gym.

"It was a resounding success!" he replies. "You got the message over loud and clear. Every woman in the Colony, at least, will vote for Marcus after that. And I suspect it might have won some votes from the blokes too. They don't like their girlfriends going through all that without some kind of reward."

The TV that night is full of the event. The reporter has interviewed people in the crowd:

An elderly woman says she has now made up her mind to vote for Marcus. "I went through two pregnancies," she recalls "I knew it was my duty. But a bit of a reward would have been nice."

A young girl says she's planning to vote for Marcus anyway. "I think he's sexy," she remarks.

A young man says he hadn't thought about the matter before. "But I guess it is very important," he adds. "I'll give my vote for Marcus."

Others say they'd like to see more of the elephant.

"It gets a message over much better than all those election slogans," one says.

The Elders decline to comment.

Colette and her elephant team hold a meeting and decide to re-enact their crusade on the Thursday afternoon just before the TV debate which is still some weeks away. Colette soon finds she has become an instant celebrity in the Colony. People come up to her in the street and congratulate her, saying they are going to vote for Marcus. "You convinced me," they say.

The Elders remain ominously silent.

Marcus arrives back from the South Coast on Tuesday, unaware of Colette and her elephant team's exploit, but it doesn't take long for him to hear about it – the topic is still on everyone's lips. He walks casually down the office aisle and speaks to Colette's supervisor. "I need to speak to Colette 850 if she's now back at work," he says in his office voice.

"Yes, of course, Sir," replies the supervisor protectively, "She was back at her desk at 8.30am yesterday, ready for work."

"Good," says Marcus, walking over to Colette's small office.

Colette looks up and sees Marcus beaming at her briefly before he resumes his office demeanour and asks her to attend to a question on energy policy. In his now customary way, he surreptitiously slips a note under her compudule and walks out.

Carefully, Colette covers her keyboard and retrieves the note. It reads:

I didn't know you played the trumpet - so much to learn about you yet! How would tomorrow at 5.15pm suit you for Pacific Avenue? I have two hours before I meet with a delegation from the North Coast. A cab can pick you up on the corner of the Esplanade at 5pm." Reply via the usual channel.

Next afternoon at 5pm a cab is waiting for her on the corner of the Esplanade and Colette is soon at 2 Pacific Avenue, her heart beating with excitement at seeing Marcus again.

Lorf and Hazel are sitting at the entrance, enjoying some cooler sea breeze. She greets them and they ask her how the election is going.

"Well..." she replies, "We're keeping our fingers crossed. Those Elders are a tough lot."

"Yes," says Lorf, "We've experienced their nasty ways over th' years. We woulda vote fer Marcus, but we don' 'ave a vote," he laments. "We is beyond th' pale."

"If Marcus wins, we'll see you all get the vote," promises Colette as she walks through into the corridor leading to the stairs to the apartment.

Marcus greets her at the door with a passionate embrace and kiss.

"My darling!" he exclaims. "I missed you dreadfully while I was away. I thought and thought about you. You did a marvellous job with your Elephant Walk!"

"Marcus, my love, I have missed you too," Colette replies as he leads her into the bedroom.

"Let me help you take off that nasty office uniform," Marcus says, "Now I can see your beautiful body," he adds, lying down beside her and stroking her cheek gently.

"Oh, Colette, you've been such a heroine. Your amazing elephant stunt looks like it has tilted the election in our favour! How can I ever repay you?"

"You could give me another kiss for a start," whispers Colette, and they made love, this time fast and furiously because they know they only have a short time before Marcus has to leave for his meeting. Afterwards, they sit briefly on the balcony, looking over a peaceful ocean, gentle waves rolling slowly into the shore and breaking into fragments of silver and white in the shallows.

"I'm planning one more Elephant Walk just before the TV election debate on the Thursday. Is that OK with you?"

"The more Elephant Walks, the merrier," Marcus says, pouring another drop of wine into Colette's glass. "Oh, roll on dratted election. Let's win and get on with things!" They clink glasses and then go down to catch the two cabs Marcus has booked.

****

Marcus and the Gully Group now go into hyper campaign mode the following day and Colette finds her role as Head of Communications is taking up more and more of her time. Marcus is dashing up and down the north and south coasts in between holding meetings with groups in the Colony whom he hopes he can persuade to vote for him. Nevertheless, he and Colette manage to keep Sundays cordoned-off from the election as much as possible and try to spend those precious idyllic warm days down at the Gully House, well away from the bustle of the Colony, and the spying eyes and cameras of the Elders. But on Tuesday December 7th, a date that is to be etched into Colette mind, Marcus tucks an alarming note under her compudule during one of his visits to her boss.

Ultra-urgent! The note begins. *Can we meet at Pacific Ave early this evening? Call a cab yourself - I'll explain why later. I'll meet you there. M.*

Startled, Colette looks up, and seeing Marcus striding past her office door, she nods briefly and then gets on with her work.

Arriving at Pacific Avenue that evening, Colette is greeted by Lorf who warns "Youse must hurry. Marcus says get inside fast!"

She scurries up the stairs to the apartment and finds the door slightly ajar. Pushing it open, she comes upon Marcus standing ready to close and lock it. He looks extremely worried.

"Colette, my darling," he gasps, wrapping his arms tightly around her. "Thank god you've come! Things are getting very serious. Come out on to the balcony and sit down and I'll explain."

Colette, intrigued and alarmed, follows him out onto the balcony. "I'm all ears," she says. "What's up?"

Marcus leans forward and grips her hand. "I've received an anonymous email," he begins, "It says: 'Beware. They're onto you and your little girlfriend. They don't have proof – yet. Take care.' It is signed 'A well-wisher'"

"You mean, the Elders have found out about us?" queries Colette, the seriousness of this starting to dawn on her.

"I always knew I was tempting fate being with you," Marcus says. "I knew I was transgressing the No.1 Colony Rule set in stone: 'No fraternising between bosses and staff in the bureaucracy'. But I couldn't hold back any longer – I desperately wanted to be with you."

Realising the seriousness of the matter, Colette sits up straight.

"Well," she says, "We simply must not provide them with any proof. If they can prove it, the whole election result is in jeopardy, and the Colony itself too!"

"Yes," Marcus agrees, "So far, they have no proof. That's why I asked you to call your cab yourself today, and why I managed to find a back way into our building here, so I wasn't spotted entering by the front. We're going to have to bite the bullet and not be together until at least after the TV debate on the Thursday before the election. We simply can't risk losing everything, no matter how much I'll miss you in the meantime. I can't let this endanger you, either. If the Elders were to win, your whole career could suffer serious setbacks if they could prove we both transgressed the Rule."

Colette agrees. "I'll miss being with you dreadfully, too," she replies, "Those lovely Sundays we've been having. But too much is at stake. It's only 16 days to the TV debate and we've both got a lot to do before then to ensure we win."

"Oh, Colette!" exclaims Marcus as he leads her into the bedroom. "One last time until the election. Let's make the most of it!"

****

The following fortnight seems to drag slowly for Colette, even though she's frantically busy. Not having any contact with Marcus cripples her, but she knows how vital it is for them not to be seen together, except in a work capacity. Marcus himself, is working very hard and there's little opportunity for either of them to even see one another in the distance. Colette is building up her communications role and is invited several times to appear on the TV news. The producer of the program is impressed by her and offers her a job.

"I'd enjoy that," Colette has replied, "But my main job is to look after my work in the Department of Big Data Verification – at least till the Election. If we win, I would be changing my job and I would love to do a regular slot about the Arts and how we can help young artists and musicians in the Colony."

"It's a deal," the producer replies. "I hope you do win."

She goes to the staff canteen every day for lunch and catches up with a lot of her old friends whom she hasn't seen since she met Marcus. They all want to know if she's planning another Elephant Walk.

"Yes," she replies, "on the Thursday, just before the big TV election debate."

Finally, on the eve of the TV debate, Colette meets Rodney and Melanie down at the old gym to check out the elephant and make final plans. "All is set," Colette decides. "Our trusty old elephant is bearing up well. Melanie, I'll leave you to get the other girls along with their placards. You and Rodney are both doing a great job. See you tomorrow around 5pm."

That night, Colette swings in her hammock and thinks about Marcus. *It has been a weird, wonderful, beautiful couple of months,* she thinks. *My whole life has changed so much. Marcus is not only the most attractive, sexy, interesting, kind, man possible, but he's also opened my eyes to a whole new world, a new stratum of society, a new way of thinking about life...* She dozes off...

****

The TV debate is to be held in the old council chambers up the road from the Beach, and Suyen has pulled out all the stops to hang VOTE MARCUS posters and balloons along the street railings. The Elders have countered the Gully Group with their own posters claiming, under a grim photo of Marcus STOP THIS CROOK KILLING OUR COLONY. The debate is to start at 7pm in time for all the people who can't get to the council chambers to see it at home on their TVs.

A large crowd has arrived at the council chambers, keen to hear the debate and to find out how the result of the election might affect their lives.

Members of the Gully Group are waiting in the big hall inside the council chambers, handing out leaflets and answering questions.

The Elders arrive, with Marmeduke, dressed in a dark suit, looking pompous as usual. They wave to the crowd and take the best seats in the front row.

"They look as if they own the place," mutters Simon. He glances at his watch. "It's 6.30. Where on earth are Marcus and co?"

As the time ticks on, the Gully Group becomes anxious. The crowd begins to get restless. They want to see Marcus and his team.

"They've got cold feet," says one of the Elders' supporters loudly. Some people laugh. Others hiss.

"I'll ring them and see where they are," Simon says, dialling. "No answer! What on earth is going on?"

Little does he realise what has been going on down the road.

Meanwhile, Colette, hoping to convert some last-minute doubters with her second Elephant Walk, has decided to try and catch the workers as they leave their offices at 5pm. As before, the roll of drums and a trumpet fanfare introduces the elephant, and soon groups of office workers on their way home wave and cheer. It is a successful sweep of the Esplanade and Rodney then turns the elephant around and they travel up a side street back to the old gym. It is 5.45pm when Rodney's phone rings. It is Suyen, her voice shaking:

"Rodney, help! This is urgent! Marcus and William and Charlie and I were having a last-minute conference in the little gatehouse next to the park near the council chambers when…" her voice cracks and she begins sobbing.

"What's happening?" demands Rodney. "tell me what has happened, Suyen!"

Suyen's voice strengthens. "Suddenly some men, wearing black masks and holding guns, broke down the door and told us to put up our hands. Then they grabbed Marcus and the others and started tying them up with rope.

"I managed to escape and I ran down to the beach. I'm now down at the police station. But the three Colony police officers aren't here. The office clerk says they've been called away by one of the Elders to an emergency up Toffs' Hill!"

THE ELEPHANT IN THE ROOM

"Stay where you are, Suyen, and I'll consult with Colette," Rodney says, turning to Colette and briefly explaining what Suyen has told him.

Colette goes white in the face and stands silent for a moment. Then she turns to Rodney:

"It's up to us to save them," she states firmly. "we don't have time to call on the Army because they're billeted away from the Colony. The police are obviously investigating a false alarm up the Hill instigated by the Elders. It's up to us.

"Get back into the elephant van, leave the girls behind except for Melanie who bangs the drums. We're going to make an infantry charge! Take the broom and whatever else you can find as weapons!"

Then they drive the elephant up the hill as fast as they can and stop just before the gatehouse.

"Now," says Colette, still in her gold tunic and standing up on the elephant like a Boadicea, "Rodney, drive the elephant right up to the door of the gatehouse. Then I'll start blowing the trumpet and Melanie will bash the drum. Then we'll charge into the gatehouse and frighten the daylights out of those thugs!"

"What if they shoot?" asks Rodney.

"They won't," Colette replies, "They'll be too stunned by the noise and commotion." The somewhat ludicrous little van and its passengers drive up to the gatehouse.

"Now charge!" shouts Colette and she blows the trumpet louder than she's ever blown it before, as they charge into the gatehouse. Inside, they find Marcus, and William and Charlie sitting on chairs, their mouths gagged, and their hands and feet tied up with rope.

The two masked men have been standing in front of them., holding their guns at the ready. but when the giant noise erupts they turn around in surprise, giving Rodney the opportunity to attack them with his broom handle. One of the men drops his gun to the floor. The other staggers sideways after being bashed on the head by Rodney, who isn't a gymnast for nothing.

"Quick!" shouts Colette, "Grab the other gun!" and Melanie picks it up and uncocks it like she's seen in the movies.

Then Rodney and Melanie rush to untie Marcus and William and Charlie. The two masked men, who are later identified as cronies of the Elders, run off. Next, Colette dismounts from the elephant outside and comes into the room.

"Quick, Marcus, you've got to get to the debate now! It's going to start in two minutes without you! The future of the election...the future of the Colony is at stake. Run!" Charlie rings the police again, and, finding them back at the police station, asks them to search for the masked men and arrest them, while Marcus and William run up the road to the Council Chambers, just in time for Marcus to climb up on to the stage and sit down in front of the TV cameras.

The debate, which isn't really a true debate, more a talk by each contender, is introduced by the moderator who stipulates that each speaker should talk for 20 minutes.

The order of speakers is to be chosen by the toss of an old antique penny salvaged from the Olden Days and taken out of the Mall Museum for the occasion.

Marmeduke wins the toss, and Marcus, still shaken by the event at the gatehouse, but managing to calm down quickly, is secretly pleased. That way, he will be able to tear Marmeduke's argument to shreds – or so he hopes. *So far, so good,* Marcus thinks as he waits for the debate to start. *Colette and I haven't given the Elders' spies any opportunity to catch us together – so they haven't a leg to stand on.*

Colette, starting to recover from the drama she's just been through, is pleased to see Marcus has taken her advice and is wearing a light-coloured suit, and he's looking relatively calm.

Marmeduke, to their consternation, speaks well and confidently, pointing out the great achievements of the Colony.

"Look what we now have, only two generations since The Calamity and The Ultimate Virus wiped out the face of the world," he says. "We have a stable society, no drug-taking, no criminal warfare, no politicians at each other's' throats for personal gain.

"We have turned out backs against the evils of The Best of Times. Our population is growing in a controlled and manageable fashion. Things are going along happily, why rock the boat?"

The audience relaxes, and some members clap. Marcus can see that Marmeduke has his audience in thrall. He, Marcus, will need to make a super-human effort to regain the trust of the audience – and the entire electorate watching the debate on TV.

Marmeduke goes on in this vein until Marcus begins to feel distinctly depressed. *What chance will I have to sway the crowd after this comforting address? People don't welcome change.*

Finally, the moderator interrupts Marmeduke, announcing: "Sir, you now have two minutes left."

Colette relaxes. *Phew! No mention of Marcus and me,* she thinks, *They couldn't get their proof.*

Marmeduke pauses and suddenly his tone of voice changes, taking on a sneering tone and his expression echoes it.

"I now have to announce a most serious matter, indeed a criminal act by my rival, Marcus 460, the Chief Administrator of this Colony," Marmeduke pauses dramatically, "He has violated a fundamental Rule of the Colony which states that no-one in authority can conduct a sexual liaison with a staff member. This is an inviolate code and it has never been breached before in the history of the Colony.

"But now, Marcus 460, the Chief Administrator, has been conducting an illicit, dirty, sneaky sexual affair with Colette 850, a junior member of the staff of the Department of Administration.

"This is rank violation of the laws of the Colony. Marcus is not fit to hold any position of authority, let alone remain Chief Administrator. He deserves to be put in gaol."

With that, Marmeduke sits down to complete silence, followed by a flutter of exclamations among members of the audience and muted applause.

Marcus, stunned by Marmeduke's surprise attack, then gets up, standing silently until the audience quietens down.

"My fellow Colonists," he begins. "I was planning to start my speech by saying that we have a sacred duty to make the human race not only survive but prosper and reach its full potential. If we don't plan for the future and start making certain important changes to the Colony, we are doomed, and the human race is doomed.

"But before I start my speech, I must address Marmeduke's evil attack and smear not only on my reputation but also that of Colette 850 who is an exemplary, indeed courageous, member of the Colony's community.

"I first noticed Colette over two years ago and was instantly attracted to her. But I was aware of the Rule against fraternisation between bosses and staff members. However, I kept an eye on her work and I became ever-more impressed by the high quality of her research and her fine mind. I remained celibate for those two years, but I finally could not resist my powerful attraction to her any longer.

"Colette and I have now been conducting an illicit love affair for the past few months. I confess this is against the Rule of the Colony, but I declare I love her dearly, more and more each day, and if I win the election and thus have a future before me, I have a plan. We don't have marriage in the Colony, but I intend to invite her to become my partner in life, and I dearly hope she will agree."

One of the Elders' supporters jeers but then someone in the audience starts to clap loudly, and someone else shouts out "Good on yer, Marcus!" and then the entire audience erupts in a burst of cheers. Sitting in the front row, Colette finds herself blushing and overwhelmed. *Marcus, my dearest,* she thinks.

"Thank you, everyone, for your support and understanding," Marcus goes on. "Indeed, one of the things I want to change if I'm elected, is to permit any boss to have sexual relations with a member of their staff – so long as the liaison is made public. This would ensure that no unfair favours could be granted by a boss to his or her partner because everybody would be aware of the relationship. People working together are bound to find one another attractive, and to discover they have common interests through their work. It's only natural that people in such circumstances might become attracted to one another. Thus, if I win the election I'll work to change the Rule -, the Rule that I myself have broken.

"And while I'm on this subject, if I win I want to make it possible for anyone – not just bosses and their staff – who has a stable relationship with someone else in the Colony to apply for a larger dwelling so they can live together comfortably."

Once again, the audience erupts in loud cheers and clapping. Several couples in the audience kiss each other in delight, while the TV cameras pan across to Marmeduke who sits slumped in his chair, silent.

THE ELEPHANT IN THE ROOM

"Now," Marcus continues. "In the brief time I have left to speak, I want to mention several other items on our – the Gully Group's – agenda." He pauses and gestures to the members of the Gully Group standing behind him.

"We want to extend the available housing for everyone – not just couples. If a small group of friends want to share a house, they, too, may apply to the Department of Housing. Indeed, single residents needing more space to carry out a hobby or interest, may also apply for larger accommodation. This cannot be done overnight, we will need to ensure the water supply is reconnected for each new residence, and that there is a sufficient solar electricity supply, and necessary repairs carried out. But we should be able to start moving people to new accommodation within a few months.

"Secondly, we want to address what Colette has so effectively highlighted: the elephant in the room. The fact that the women of the Colony have selflessly undergone pregnancy in order to increase the population methodically – with no reward – is shocking, and indeed they have been penalised by being held back a year on their promotion ladder. We intend to put this glaringly unfair situation to rights immediately after the election, if we win. We also want to reward the Nannies who have done such a selfless task looking after us all as babies and children.

Once again, the audience cheers and claps and hoots approval.

"We have long-term plans to deal with the need for a new legal system, a constitution, and many other matters, such as setting up an apprentice system, not only for trades but also for professions such as medicine, engineering, IT, pharmacy – to ensure we have enough trained people. . But these matters will take longer for us to sort out.

"Meanwhile, we want to start at once to encourage Colonists to take up farming so that we can be sure of a proper food supply as our population grows.

"We need to start making things ourselves, too, instead of relying on what we have scrounged from the shops and warehouses and empty houses. The batteries we use will eventually get too old to use. We also need to find oil and other, extra, sources of electricity, and we need to follow in the

105

footsteps of the first colonists back in the late 18th century and early 19th century who crossed the Mountains and opened up the great farming land to the West.

"Above all, I want to give everybody more of a say in the vital decisions that affect us all.

"And we want this Colony, which has developed from babyhood, to childhood, to adolescence, to have the chance to reach full adulthood, and to prosper. We want to learn from the mistakes our forebears made, and not repeat them, but we also want to celebrate the best things the human race is capable of.

"We have been given a second chance. Let us grasp that precious chance and make the very best of it!"

Marcus then sits down amid a frenzy of cheers.

The moderator takes the microphone and thanks both the speakers and reminds everyone that it is compulsory to vote in the election the next day. "This was the custom, dating from the Olden Days in this country, and though it had its faults, it provided a much more stable government than most of the other countries in the world." The moderator announces, adding that if anyone watching at home is ill or seriously unable to attend one of the polling booths, they should call the Electoral Office and one of the polling booth supervisors will visit their home with a ballot paper. With that, the event ends, and people start trailing out into the evening. Some stay behind to congratulate Marcus.

"Good luck tomorrow," one says. "Barring accidents you should win by a country mile!"

Finally, Marcus and Marmeduke step down from the platform. Marmeduke slinks off by a side door, while Colette and the Gully Group rush up to Marcus and embrace him. Marcus, flushed and exhausted, gives Colette a special kiss and suggests they all go down the beachfront to cool off and somehow get hold of something to eat and drink.

As they walk back down the hill to the beach, Marcus holds Colette's hand. "My darling, I am so proud to be holding your hand in public," he says.

"Marcus, I simply love you," is all Colette can say.

They all sit down at a picnic table under the Norfolk pines and recall the highlights of the debate.

106

THE ELEPHANT IN THE ROOM

"Marcus, my heart was in my mouth when you confessed about your affair," William says. "But you carried if off superbly, and from then on you had the audience with you."

"Well, I had to refute Marmeduke's snide attack and I wanted to protect Colette," Marcus replies. "Now I'll go and see if I can scrounge up some food and drink for all of us. Let's hope someone feels moved to start a restaurant down here before too long!"

While Marcus is away on his food hunt, Rodney comes and sits down next to Colette. "Colette," he begins, "I want to congratulate you and Marcus. You are obviously made for one another – you'll spark off each other forever!

"I'm glad, too, that I now know the real reason you split from me. I thought I'd hurt your feelings, or done something wrong, but now I realise you had experienced love at first sight."

"Yes," agrees Colette, "a '*coup de foudre*,' as they say in books."

Colette looks at Rodney and puts her hand on his arm.

"Dear, dear, Rodney, I enjoyed being with you and I know we will always be close friends. I know I can trust you, and I know that if ever I was in trouble, you would come to my rescue. And I would do the same for you. Are you happy with Melanie? She's a very good person."

"Yes," Rodney replies, "Mel is a very sweet and loving girl. I can really relax with her – she doesn't bring up complicated topics like you! But I'll never forget my time with you."

Marcus arrives back, carrying some bottles and a large carry-bag. "This is the best I could scrounge from the central kitchen," he announces, "but at least we won't starve."

After drinks are poured, Charlie stands up and raises his glass.

"I want to make a toast to Marcus: You did us proud tonight! Congratulations on a great speech!'

They all raise their glasses and let out a cheer.

"And now," Charlie continues, "I want to congratulate you, Marcus and Colette, we wish you a very happy future together!"

At the end of a lively repast, Colette, starting to feel weary after such a momentous day, gets up to leave, bidding the Gully Group goodnight.

107

Marcus walks her back to her apartment building.

"Colette," he suggests as they reach the front door of the building, "could we spend tomorrow and Sunday, Christmas Day, at 2 Pacific Avenue? If we win the Election tomorrow, we can celebrate there. And if we lose, we can commiserate together."

"Of course, that would be lovely!" says Colette. "But is it really liveable yet?"

"Well, the water's now on, and so is the electricity. I've had the whole place thoroughly cleaned by the Department of Housing cleaners, and – I hope you don't mind my doing this – I've put down some oriental rugs in the main rooms. I wanted you to help me choose all the furnishings, but the rugs happened to be available at the depot, so I grabbed them.

"But I want you to have a look at some photos of sofas and chairs and other furniture I saw at the depot, and if you like some of them, I can get them delivered tomorrow, just in time for Christmas."

They embrace farewell and Colette goes upstairs to her solitary hammock. Tomorrow is the Election and she sorely needs some sound sleep.

16

ELECTION DAY

VOTING COMMENCES at 9am in the Colony and will finish at 6pm, while the hamlets up-and-down the South and North Coast start voting at 7am to finish at 4pm to allow the fast electric courier bikes time to pick up all the votes and transport them back to the central polling station in the Colony to be counted for the poll result to be announced by 11.30pm.

Suyen has set up Gully Group stands at the polling booths in three areas of the Colony: up the Mall, down the beachfront, and outside the old Council Chambers where the debate had been held the previous day. She has organised a tribe of helpers to hand out How to Vote cards.

Marcus calls at Colette's apartment to pick her up and accompany her to the polling station down the beach. "How are you feeling?" she asks Marcus as they stroll down the footpath, again luxuriating in the sensation of holding hands in public.

"Well, naturally I feel nervous. But deep down I think we might win. You've done a great deal to help with your Elephant Walks; they sent a definite buzz through the community."

As they approach the polling booth, the TV crew film them and then come up to Marcus and ask how he felt about the election.

"Too early to tell," he replies

Marcus and Colette are both filmed casting their votes and then they walk out to the sea front and sit down on a bench. A soft breeze is feathering the waves. It promises to be a hot day, in the high-30s.

"Now," Marcus says, "We've got the whole day ahead of us. Let's go over to Pacific Avenue and start sorting out the furnishings."

Arriving a No 2 Pacific Avenue, they come across Lorf sitting in the sun mending his fishing rod. "One day, Lorf, I'd like to accompany you on one of your fishing expeditions. I think you could teach me a thing or two about how to catch a fish," Marcus says.

"Be glad t'ave youse along," replies Lorf, knotting a length of line together and tightening the knot with his teeth.

"I haven't seen Hazel around much the last few days," Colette remarks.

"Na, the old 'Aze ain't feelin' too crash 'ot. In fact she's real crook," replies Lorf. "We think it musta been some old 'amburger meat we got outta one'v the bins down th' beach."

"How did you get through the Wire?" asks Marcus.

"Not sayin'," replies Lorf, spitting onto the pavement.

"Well, let us know if we can bring her some stomach medicine or something," Colette suggests. She's about to remark that it's bad luck Hazel is ill at Christmas, when she bites her tongue. *Of course, it is unlikely that Lorf and his mates would have the resources to celebrate Christmas.*

Marcus and Colette then go up to the apartment and Marcus shows Colette the improvements that have been made since she was last there on that traumatic day when they decided they would have to stay apart until after the TV debate. "Look!" he says, pressing a switch, "Electricity!" and, going into the kitchen, he turns on the tap and water flows out into a gleaming sink. Colette looks around the kitchen and notices that everything is polished and clean. The fridge door has been repaired, as has the electric stove. On the bench is a state-of-the-art coffee machine, the kind Sophie had mentioned in her diary towards the end of The Best of Times. Next, Colette peeps into her bathroom – Marcus has a separate one – and, opening the bathroom cupboard, she finds neatly arranged on the shelves an array of luxury shampoos, face-and body-creams, perfumes, and brushes and combs. "How did you know what to put in my bathroom?" Colette calls out to Marcus.

"Karla taught me a thing or two about what women like," Marcus calls back. Colette smiles to herself.

"And what's this weird thing that looks a bit like a large gun, hanging on the wall?" she asks.

"That 'thing'," Marcus replies, laughing, "is a hair-dryer. Haven't you seen one before?"

ELECTION DAY

"No," says Colette. "You'll have to show me how to use it. We ordinary Colonists don't run to such luxuries."

Marcus, on hearing this, looks serious for a moment. *Hmmm*, he ponders to himself, *I didn't realise how big a gap has already developed between the managers and the workers in the Colony. Something must be done about it.*

Colette then goes on to admire the rest of the apartment. The marble floor gleams, the walls have been repainted white, the windows and sliding doors cleaned so the ocean seems almost to be breaking in over the balcony railing. And in the main bedroom is a handsome king-size bed, complete with pure Irish linen sheets and pillowcases, with the old oriental cover folded over it.

"What a marvellous bed!" she exclaims, flopping onto it and bouncing up-and-down. "Although," she smiles, looking up at Marcus, who is standing in the doorway, "I'll always have a special soft spot for our old inflatable mattress!"

Next, Marcus shows her photographs he's taken of various items of furniture. "You choose," he says. "I've done enough on my own."

What Colette then chooses pleases Marcus. "Our tastes are very similar," he says. "thank goodness."

"Well you didn't think I'd want purple and orange floral sofa covers, did you?" she shoots back.

He orders the furniture, and a TV, and is told by the central warehouse that everything will arrive in two hours' time, just before lunch.

"Let's go down for a swim now, while we wait for the furniture to arrive," he suggests.

Colette has worn her bikini under her shirt and trousers, so they go down the beach in a flash. They dive in-and-out of the breaking waves, rolling over in the shallows together. There's quite a lot of seaweed about that day, but Marcus doesn't toss it at Colette. *He's not a tossing seaweed kind of person, thank goodness*, she observes.

Back at the apartment, the furniture arrives dead on time.

"I guess one of the perks about being Chief Administrator is that things get delivered on time," Colette teases him.

"It might well be my last perk," says Marcus soberly, suddenly remembering the election. "Maybe it'll be

111

Marmeduke's turn tomorrow. And I might well be on my way, handcuffed, to the outer regions of the Colony, banished forever."

Colette gives him a hug and a back rub. "You'll win," she sooths. "I feel it in my bones."

They spend a couple of hours choosing where to put the furniture, and finally the apartment looks simply beautiful, and Colette and Marcus collapse happily on to their big new bed. They are soon discovering yet further new things to enjoy together, and we will leave them in peace and privacy for the moment.

It is 6pm when they awake and get ready for the election result up at the old council chambers. Before they set off, Marcus gives Colette a box wrapped with Christmas paper.

"This is a pre-Christmas gift," he explains. "Maybe you'd like to wear it – briefly – when we get back here after the party. It'll be our first entire night together."

Colette unwraps the parcel to find an elegant cream satin nightgown. She lays it out on the bed and hugs Marcus again.

They set off on foot, up to the Wire, passing through the security gate before walking up to the council chambers where some of the polling booth workers are already opening drinks, while the officials are busily counting votes. It is still too early for any reliable exit poll results and there's a nervous tension in the air.

Colette and Marcus go to the large room where the post-election party had already begun. A small band is playing, and the Gully Group and their friends are standing at one end of the room, while the Elders have stationed themselves at the other end.

"Ne'r the twain shall meet," remarks William, who is of a literary bent.

The room is decorated with the balloons and streamers of the opposing parties and there's an uncomfortable frisson between the two groups until Marcus strides over and shakes Marmeduke's hand.

"May the best man and the best team win," he says. "But while we wait for the result, let's enjoy the party." Marmeduke grunts and reluctantly shakes Marcus's hand.

ELECTION DAY

By 7.30pm, the exit poll results are showing a favourable swing to the Gully Group, but Marcus refuses to celebrate just yet. "We still need the results from the Hill, and they're likely to be very pro-Elders," he points out. "And we don't really know how the country vote will be until all their votes arrive to be counted."

At one stage Colette bumps into Alistair, whom she hasn't seen since Karla's party. She notices an expression of disdain pass over his features, but she's determined to do something to ease the situation.

"Alistair," she says, "I really enjoyed our conversation about German art. We must meet again before too long. I'd like to quiz you on your knowledge of French art too. I suspect you are also an expert on that!" Alistair's expression softens – Colette is right in thinking he's susceptible to flattery.

Colette then re-joins the Gully Group and tells Marcus she needs to go back to her old apartment to pick up some things she's forgotten. He hails a cab for her and she's soon back, carrying a suitcase, in time for the election result.

Finally, it's 11.30pm. The band delivers a drum roll and the TV compere takes the microphone.

"And now," announces the compere, "we have the results of the very first Election this Colony has ever held!"

The drums roll again.

"The results are, 20 per cent of the vote to…the Elders…And the winner is …" he pauses dramatically, "Marcus and the Gully Group! Marcus has won 80 per cent of the vote, leaving 20 per cent to the Elders."

The drums roll again.

"Come up to the microphone and cameras, Marcus," the compere calls.

Marcus stands in front of the microphone for a minute while the cheers die down.

"Thank you all," he says, pointing first to the Gully Group, and then to the other voters in the room, "the Gully Group and its helpers have done me proud. And thank you to those who voted for us. This is an historic moment for our Colony, the first step in the Colony's growth to adulthood.

"We have a mammoth task before us, but we will succeed. As far as we know, we are the only humans left on earth. We have been given a second chance to get things right this time. So let's get on with it!"

The room erupts in a roar of cheers.

The Elders decline to speak.

Marcus goes around the Gully Group thanking them all personally.

"We need to have a meeting the day after tomorrow – Boxing day – at the beach Pavilion," he says. "Much has to be planned. See you there at 11am. We'll have a celebration barbecue in the park and then it's back to work!" Marcus and Colette then walk towards the beach, go through the gate in the Wire and down to their apartment, passing by Lorf's gang, sound asleep beside their smouldering fire.

"I've got them a bag of fresh hamburgers and Christmas cake which I'll give them tomorrow for Christmas lunch," Marcus says as they climb the stairs. "And I've organised a twice-weekly drop-off of fresh bread rolls and fresh sausages for them from now on. I can't bear the thought of them scrounging around the rubbish bins for old scraps. Poor old Hazel is certainly not very well as a result of their scavenging."

Upstairs in the apartment, Marcus and Colette walk out and sit on the balcony for a while, recovering from the day's events. A full moon is shining down across the sea, its golden path heading straight towards them.

"Colette," Marcus says, putting his arm around her. "At the TV debate I said that if I won the election I'd invite you to become my partner in life. Will you?"

Colette turns and kisses him.

"Of course," is all she needs to say. And with that, they retire to their bedroom.

17

CHRISTMAS SURPRISES

CHRISTMAS DAY. The weather has turned cool and cloudy. A soft mist hangs over the ocean as Colette and Marcus lie together in bed, dreamily thinking about the day ahead.

"Marcus," says Colette, "I have a little Christmas gift for you. I'm not eligible on my grade in the Department to have access to the luxury warehouse, so I can't give you something glamorous. The best present I can give you is just something I've been collecting all my life."

She gets up and goes to the wardrobe where she had put her suitcase. Opening it, she takes out a stack of narrow boxes and brings them back to the bed where Marcus has plumped up the pillows and is sitting up against them.

Laying the boxes out on the bed, Colette opens the first one. Inside is a row of seashells, opalescent in the morning light.

Marcus catches his breath. "They're simply magnificent!" he exclaims, holding up a large conch shell to his ear. "I can hear the sea," he murmurs, "It's even louder than the sea outside."

They open the rest of the boxes, picking up a rainbow-hued shell here and a tortoiseshell-patterned one there, and Colette explains she has been collecting them from the beach since she could first walk. "My Nanny used to bring me down to the beach and I'd wander off to find shells. Some of them were washed up from other places to the north of the Colony, others I found when I was old enough to climb over the rocks to the rock pools around the point."

"I cannot think of a more precious present!" Marcus exclaims, kissing her again. "It's far, far better than any luxury gift. I will treasure this shell collection for the rest of my life."

Marcus is overcome by Colette's gift. *What a funny, funny, lovely girl*, he muses. *She's so capable, and so extroverted, so good with people – and yet she's also so vulnerable and sensitive. I feel honoured that she feels she can show that vulnerable side to me. Like many very intelligent people, she spends most of her time shielding her true self. She's learned how to behave and act like everyone else, to be "normal", but inside her is that precious sensitivity. I love her dearly.*

Then he gives her a small box.

This is for you, Colette. Merry Christmas and many, many, many Happy New Years!"

Colette opens the little box to find a simple gold ring inside.

"You'll need this to read the inscription on the inner side of the ring," he says, handing her a magnifying glass.

Colette peers inside the ring to see the words engrave on it: "To Colette, my life partner, love Marcus."

"Next," Marcus says, "let me slip this ring on your finger with my promise to honour my pledge to you as my life partner." They sat in silent communion for a minute or two.

"And now," he says, swinging his legs down to the floor "let's get up and have breakfast. I know it's Christmas Day, but I want to go down and explore the car park under these apartments, and then I want to take you to see a house."

"Not another house!" exclaims Colette.

"Yes, a rather special house," Marcus says. "I think you'll understand why I want you to see it, when you get there."

Taking a box of tools with him, Marcus leads the way down to the entrance while Colette carries the bag of Christmas hamburgers and cake to give to Lorf. Marcus tells Lorf the hamburgers and cake are a repayment for guarding their apartment from evil-doers. "No prob," says Lorf, accepting the gift. "What youse got them tools for?"

Marcus explains they want to go down to what had once been the Residents' car park to inspect the garage belonging to their apartment.

"Well in that case youse 'ad betta take one 'a these clubs and one 'a them long bitsa wood with yer." Lorf advises. "There's wild dogs and feral cats and possums and all kinda nasty critters down in car park."

So well-armed, Marcus and Colette venture down some stairs to the car park. Fortunately, Marcus has brought a torch, for it's fiendishly dark down there as they push their way through accumulated debris. Small animals, probably rats, scuttle under their feet and then a dog barks, followed by another. Soon the car park echoes to a cacophony of wild barking, and Colette and Marcus can just make out in the torchlight a weird array of mixed dog breeds – large Great Dane-bull terriers, small part-poodle-part corgis, ferociously-fanged Rottweiler-pit-bull crosses – the mongrel descendants of the pampered pooches that had belonged to the rich living in Bondi in The Best of Times.

"Be very careful, Colette, don't for god's sake let them come near you. If they bite, you might get rabies!" Marcus warns, as he lashes out at the dogs with his club and long stick. They reach Garage Number 2, and Marcus, moving as fast as he can, wrenches open its door whose electronic opening device had long ago rusted away. "Quick, Colette, come inside the garage and we'll close down the door!" shouts Marcus as the yapping dogs come closer.

Inside the dark garage, Marcus's torch lights up a sleepy fruit bat which has somehow got inside.

"Don't go near it either," he warns Colette. "They carry rabies too. In fact, that's probably how the dogs get infected nowadays. They also carry dangerous viruses." Then he shines the torch onto a large, sturdily-built car. "It must have been the vehicle left behind by Sophie when she fled the impending Calamity and travelled in the furniture van to the house in the Mountains.

"This is a very interesting car," Marcus adds, peering under its bonnet. "It's a hybrid electric-petrol vehicle, a rarity by the 2030s. I'll get Charlie's mechanics to get it out of here and taken down to the Gully House for repairs. It might well come in useful for my longer country trips where the roads are extremely rutted and bumpy and there aren't many battery-charger depots along the way."

Meanwhile, Colette has poked around too and has located a trunk. "Maybe this might contain something interesting," she suggests, pointing it out to Marcus.

"Perhaps," he replies. "But we'll have to leave that for another day. I'll ask Charlie's men to remove it along with the car. We need to get out of this hell-hole now, safe-and-sound. Get ready to rush to the door when I say 'Go'!"

They just manage to escape back to the entrance of the building, with a yowling pack of dogs behind them, and give back Lorf's club and stick.

"Ta," Lorf says, "I may be need'n 'em t'night. One of them gangs is due."

"But I thought most of the gang members had died by now," Marcus says.

"Na, new gen'rashun's comin' from the country parts," Lorf replies. "Theys young an' tough." Marcus frowns at this. Something would have to be done to protect Lorf and his ageing gang – and his and Colette's precious apartment, let alone the Colony itself.

"How's Hazel?" he asks.'

"Still bloody crook," replies Lorf. Marcus asks if he could do anything to help, but Lorf shakes his head.

"Na," he replies. "She'll probly get over it."

Marcus then calls a cab to take them to the Gully, and before they get in, he warns Colette: "Be careful what you say in this cab. All the cabs are wired and connected to the digital system set up by the Elders. William's first job now is to dismantle and deactivate that spy network. So I shan't discuss anything of importance till we arrive at our destination. We might have won the election, but we still have enemies."

The cab is about to turn down the road into the Gully when Marcus commands it to stop and wait for them at the wrought-iron gates of a very old sandstone house which Colette hasn't noticed before. They get out and Marcus pulls out a set of keys and opens the gate and they walk towards the house up a curved gravel drive through what must have been a splendid garden with trellises now overgrown, and garden beds choked with weeds. The house is long and low, one-storey, with a wide veranda running along the front on each side of a central entrance with double shutters across the doorway. The roof is slate, and, as they step onto the veranda, Colette observes it's tiled with beautiful geometric mosaic tiles in deep blue and white with touches of pink. Before going inside, Marcus suggests they sit down on a wooden seat on the veranda.

"I'll tell you what I've found out about this place," he says, taking an old brochure out of his pocket. "It's called Bronte House. I discovered its history in the records in the council chambers of what had been Waverley Council, which used to caretake the house back in The Best of Times.

"It's a truly historic colonial house, dating way back to 1832 when its building work was started by the New South Wales Colonial Architect, Mortimer Lewis," he reads from the brochure.

"I think this house could become the official residence of the head of the Colony, whatever the head will eventually be called, but probably the 'President.'"

"I will probably eventually become the first President once the constitution is sorted out, and I would like to have this place dedicated to the Colony, to be owned by the Colony – a bit like the Americans' White House used to be back in the Olden Days."

Colette is impressed, but hesitant: "But would you want to live here?" she asks.

"No, it's far too grand for my taste – as you'll see when we go inside. I wouldn't feel comfortable with all that old furniture. It's too formal for nowadays living. You'll be First Lady, would you want to live here?" Colette shakes her head.

"But it would be an ideal place for meetings of the cabinet, and for receptions for visiting regional leaders and so on."

After a careful inspection of its grand interior with its hallway of portraits of great early settlers and politicians, Marcus locks up the house and they take their cab on the short drive down to Marcus' Gully House where they sit at a little table under a tall grey-gum where Marcus has set up a barbecue.

While the meat sizzles, Marcus opens the bottle of wine and pours two glasses.

"Here's to us and to the future of the Colony," he says, and they clink glasses.

"We have some big things to sort out very quickly," he begins. "At the meeting tomorrow I'll outline these matters and discuss what we should do, but I want to get your input now."

"The most pressing matter," he goes on, "is what to do about the defeated Elders. They've had a total grip on the Colony for two generations. At the outset they had been good and honourable people, but their descendants have now degenerated into power-crazed fascists, and in defeat they might well become exceedingly dangerous – Alistair and Marmeduke in particular."

Colette agrees. She has been thinking about this too. "Alistair," she says, "is ultimately the more dangerous because he's more intelligent than Marmeduke..."

"I honestly don't know what should be done about Marmeduke," she confesses. "But I do have some suggestions about Alistair."

She goes on to explain that however dangerously intelligent he is, she believes Alistair could, with a lot of flattery, be rendered innocuous. Indeed, he might even be of use to the budding Colony.

"How?" inquires Marcus.

"Well," Colette says. "If we are the only humans left on earth, we need to ensure that the great heritage of art, music and literature created by thousands of years of human activity isn't lost to posterity.

"Alistair is uniquely knowledgeable about such matters. He could be cajoled into taking on the role of Cultural Curator for the Colony, running exhibitions and talks and even encouraging future works of art too. If he were to take on this role he would be eligible to keep his house up the Hill, which would deflect any malice towards you. I know he has acted badly, but he's containable. I might be able to get this message over to him. As you know, I got on well with Alistair at Karla's party."

"You certainly did!" laughs Marcus. "I began to fear for your safety!"

Colette continues. "I think I might be able to flatter him into submission."

They agree that this might solve the problem of Alistair, but what about Marmeduke? "I'm at my wits' end about him," Marcus confesses. "He and his cronies, despite losing so thoroughly, could well stir up a lot of trouble. That little scuffle at the gatehouse was bad enough! I'll bring the matter up at tomorrow's meeting and see what the others might suggest."

"I want to bring up some of the major things we face:

"But, as I've says before, as time goes on, some of the precious things we've salvaged will wear out. We'll start to run out of items such as clothing too, as the population increases. We'll need to make new things, and that will require raw materials which we'll need to mine for metals and drill for oil. Of course, if we can resuscitate 3D printing, a lot of items of all kinds could be manufactured quite easily. There are quite a few small workshops out in the old business parks equipped with 3D printers we can use, but we will need materials such as plastic for that. Maybe we can melt down some materials to re-use for 3-D printing. Of course, if it does turn out that there are other people still alive elsewhere – China must surely have a few souls left out of their billions – we might be able to trade with them. But there hasn't been a squeak yet out of China.

"We need to work out a way of allowing people to move into larger dwellings without creating a class-ridden society." Colette, sighs. "I think you are being idealistic," she says. "Human nature won't change. But at least we can try to do good things." The cicadas begin to thrum and the wine is beginning to take its toll.

"So much to do. Our meeting tomorrow with the victorious Gully Group will be important." murmurs Marcus.

He puts out the fire in the grate and they bundle the plates and glasses into a basket and wander lazily back into the house and up to Marcus's bedroom, where they make lazy warm afternoon love.

18

A TITANIC BATTLE

TOWARDS EVENING Marcus calls another cab to take them back to Pacific Avenue.

"We can have a quiet night there before we start work next day," Marcus says.

Little does he envisage what is in store for them that night.

They arrive back at Pacific Avenue to find Lorf sitting outside on his decrepit chair, looking morose.

"What's wrong, Lorf?" asks Colette.

"The old 'Aze is still crook, real crook," Lorf replies.

"We could get a doctor over to have a look at her," Marcus suggests. "My sister Annie's a doctor."

"Thanks," replies Lorf. "If she ain't better by the mornin' I'll take up yer offer."

Colette and Marcus go up to their apartment, concerned at the news about Hazel.

"Getting Annie around to have a look at her is about the best we can do," Marcus says. "We don't have the right to interfere too much in Lorf's set-up. He and his gang have survived perfectly well in their own way long before we came along. It'd be patronising of us to try to change their lives too much – apart from supplying them with some decent food. Anyway, it's about time you met Annie."

Marcus goes into his gleaming kitchen and starts cooking a light meal. Colette can hear him humming – cooking keeps him calm. She, meanwhile, slips into her bathroom, runs a hot bath and relaxes – she has no interest in cookery, having only ever known meals arriving on her conveyer belt and in the canteen, until she meets Marcus. After dinner, they sit out on the balcony, watching the still almost full moonlight dancing over the waves, and discuss further what needs to be done with the Colony now Marcus is officially the elected Chief Administrator.

A TITANIC BATTLE

They continue to sit on the balcony, looking out over the sea which has turned a deep indigo. Just as they get up to go inside, Marcus pricks up his ears at the sound of tramping feet and loud guttural voices coming from up the road.

"Quick!" he warns, "It's the wild Outlander gang Lorf says might be coming! I'll go down to help Lorf and his men. Colette, go into the kitchen and get out as many buckets and large saucepans as you can find. Bring them back to this balcony and start filling them with water from the tap here. Test what the water pressure in the hose is.

"You stay up here, turn off all the lights, and be ready to throw down buckets of water onto them as soon as you hear me shout. If the water pressure is up to scratch, you can hose them too."

Colette, startled, races into the kitchen and begins getting out buckets and saucepans.

Marcus, meanwhile, tucks his trusty revolver into the pocket of his shorts and takes a large broom down to the entrance of the building where he finds Lorf and his men already armed with long sticks and clubs, at the ready. The women are huddled in the far corner, obviously accustomed to attacks from marauding gangs.

"This is gonna be a big'un," Lorf announces. "Looks like it's the new gang of young'uns."

Down Pacific Avenue come about 50 large, hulking young Outlander men wearing ragged clothing, shouting and brandishing heavy clubs, iron bars, large rocks and pieces of masonry taken from collapsed buildings in the city. The battle begins, and Marcus soon finds himself in the thick of it, bashing the intruders with his broom, helping to make a path for Lorf's hardened warriors to get to the front. Lorf's men arrange themselves into a frontline, battling wave-after-wave of country louts whose massive arms and gigantic thighs act as battering rams against the older, frailer, yet-battle-hardened denizens of 2 Pacific Avenue.

Looking up at their balcony, Marcus shouts out: "Colette, first buckets!" And Colette hurls down a small torrent of water from two buckets onto the heads of the leading gang warriors. The water treatment slows the invasion momentarily, and Marcus calls out: "Keep the water coming!"

Meanwhile, Lorf's men are fighting for their lives. The young invaders are very strong. Lorf has arranged his men into three fronts. The first is in the frontline, the second stands in the street, barring the entrance to the building, while the third is stationed just inside the entrance to the garage, holding shields made from garbage tin lids. Behind them, some of the stronger women have lit a fire and are preparing red-hot sticks to hand to the men to hurl at the invaders.

Marcus grapples with one hefty invader after another. One of them clouts him over the head with an iron bar, causing him to stagger. "You bastard!" shouts Marcus, lunging back at him and grabbing him by the throat. The young man struggles to escape Marcus's grip, but Marcus is determined to throttle him, clutching him around the neck. Then he pulls him to the ground and kicks the young invader in the balls – hard. Tossing the youth out of the way into the gutter, Marcus returns to the fray. Meanwhile, Colette continues to fill her buckets and saucepans, and then she turns the hose on the battle scene below. Fortunately, the water pressure is strong.

Marcus, his head pounding from the blow from the iron bar, begins to fear that Lorf and his men are going to lose the battle. Things look dire, but the fire sticks made by the old women start to turn the tide of the attack. Coupled with litres of water being hurled down on them, the combination of fire and water begins to distract the young invaders, while Lorf and his men wield their clubs and sticks mightily. Marcus, observing that the battle is now turning in Lorf's favour, staggers back inside the entrance, reeling from the blow to his head. Slowly, he manages to climb back up the stairs and reach the apartment. Hearing him, Colette rushes to the door and helps him to lie down on the bed. Then she runs to the bathroom and soaks some hand-towels in cold water and applies them to Marcus' head.

"Make sure the front door is bolted," Marcus groans. "Those bastards might try and come up here." Colette secures the door and then returns to the bedroom, closes the shades on the sliding doors and then turns a bed light on so she can inspect his wounds.

"You aren't bleeding," she reports, "But you're going to have a mighty bruise on your forehead by tomorrow. You're lucky they didn't break your nose." She continues to apply cold water compresses until Marcus begin to fall into a fitful sleep.

"I'll just go out and see how the battle's progressing," Colette says, returning with the news that the worst appears to be over. "There are quite a few men from both sides, lying in the gutter, maybe even dead," she reports. "But the rest of the young gang are retreating up the road. Lorf has won.

"You did your bit," says Marcus wearily.

"Now go to sleep," Colette admonishes, "You've had quite enough " for one day. That was certainly some Christmas! I'll put away my Christmas nightgown for another night."

19

THE GULLY GROUP GETS GOING

MARCUS AWAKES next morning with a sore head, but otherwise none-the-worse from his encounter with the gang the previous night.

Colette has actually managed to boil him an egg successfully and has made toasted "soldiers" for him to dip. "That's the limit to my cooking abilities," she confesses. "Cooking is not my forte."

Marcus smiles. "I guess it's in my DNA, I bet Jim cooked. Your other accomplishments more than make up for any inability in the culinary domain," he adds "and I wouldn't want any competition in that respect anyway."

Although it's Boxing Day, a declared holiday in the Colony, Marcus has decided that he would hold his first meeting with his "inner cabinet", his trusty Gully Group, down in the old Pavilion, a little way along the Esplanade from the main admin building. He has had it cleaned and it will make an ideal centre for the new departments he is creating. Moreover, it isn't hooked up to the Elders' old spy network which William and his team are already starting to carefully dismantle.

As the Gully Group enters the big upstairs room in the Pavilion, overlooking the ocean, they're surprised to see the large bruise on Marcus' forehead.

"I'll explain later," he replies, taking his seat at the head of the table. "We'll discuss it when we get to Charlie.

"Now," he begins, "Let's get down to business. We have much to do if we want this Colony not merely to survive, but to prosper. I have picked each of you because I discerned in you that vital spark of intelligence, determination, ability, expertise, and above all, that awareness of the importance of human life and *joie de vivre* – I can't find a single word to describe this, but I can

126

discern it in a person if they possess it. Sadly, most people lack that quality.

"That's enough praise. You all know from the election campaign the big issues that need to be confronted, solved and enacted. You'll all be involved, one way or another, in these very important matters.

"But first of all, we must start today with the most urgent things that need to be sorted out at once. As you see, I have a bit of a bump on my forehead. This is the result of a confrontation with a new type of gang."

Marcus describes the young Outlander men from distant country areas where, in many cases, they had grown up parentless and had drifted into the city to survive.

"They are devoid of any education and have probably scavenged for food all their lives. Now they are grown men, strong and wild

"We could hunt them down and throw them into a gaol, but that wouldn't achieve much," Marcus says, "Or maybe we could round them up and put them in the Army to have discipline drilled into them and to make them work, like the convicts in the first colony in the Very Olden Days, on repairing the roads. Some of them might eventually emerge as fine soldiers. You never know, a strong army might just come in handy in the future.

"Charlie, I'd like to have your thoughts on this."

Charlie stands up, a gleam of ambition in his eyes. This is a great idea, he says. He wants to meet with Lorf that very afternoon to find out what the old man knows of the whereabouts of the various gangs. "We'll round up the lot of them," Charlie vows, "and set them to honest work."

Marcus then continues round the table: Suyen, to set up a market economy in the Colony.

- Phil to supervise the new housing allocations.
- Rodney, as Head of the new Department of Sport and Recreation, to set up a program of sporting events.
- Simon, the farmer, to expand the agricultural program. And explore the farming land on the western side of the Mountains,

- Charlie and the Army to get the main roads repaired all the way to the Western Plains and to resuscitate the former astro-telescope out on the Plains
- William to dismantle the Elders' spy network, and become the Head of IT and Telecommunications?"
- Colette, Communications and Culture

"I'd like to co-opt Melanie into my department, for a start," Colette says. "She's very bright and was extremely useful during the election campaign." She notices Rodney nodding as she says that. Then she asks if she might make a further suggestion.

"I'd like to see every one of the women who went through the pregnancy program to also receive a gift of an evening outfit of their choice from the Luxury warehouse. And then I'd like to hold a Colony Ball where all these women can wear their finery. It would be a good way of demonstrating that the new Marcus-Gully Group regime means business."

The Gully Group cheers at this plan, and Marcus adds it to his agenda.

Finally, Marcus turns to Alice sitting quietly, gazing at the meeting through her horn-rimmed spectacles. "Alice. I'm leaving the matter of drawing up a Constitution and a legal system to you and your team. You will be the head of the Legal Department and you may call on the assistance of anyone in the Colony with legal knowledge, even some of the Elders who weren't part of Alistair and Marmeduke's group. I think you should be aware that I'm beginning to think that the old system of States didn't work too well as time went on. It set regions with rivers that spanned State boundaries at loggerheads with each other. Better, perhaps, to have a Constitution based on regions, not states. And make it politician-proof!" Alice, too, is enthusiastic in her quiet, reliable way.

"That leaves three new Departments yet to have heads," Marcus says: "Education, Health, and a very important one: Manufacturing. I have a few people in mind for these tasks and I'll get your input about them in due course." Marcus then stands up. "I'm now leaving the organisation of this Pavilion building of new departments to all of you. Go and choose your offices

– there are plenty of rooms. Get whatever office equipment you need from the Department of Employment, and from William. Find your staff and get on with it. We'll have another meeting in a week's time, after New Year – same place, same time.

"I myself, will remain in the old Department of Administration building, at least for the moment. I will need to sort out a lot of people there, many of whom still owe allegiance to the Elders, who bestowed all manner of perks on them. I'll be the old, strict Marcus when I'm in that building, wearing my glasses and creating fear and obedience. But here, I can be the Marcus you've all come to know – the real Marcus."

The Gully Group clap again. "And at lunchtime we'll hold a celebratory barbecue in the park that runs down to the beach at the south end."

Marcus then turns to Colette, "Your first job is to send out a Media Release to the TV station and the radio station announcing the new appointments, including your own. I will ring the head of the Department of Employment tomorrow and set in motion the promotion by one year of all women who have been through the Pregnancy Program and by two years if they have been through the program twice. Then you can send out a second Media Release to that effect, and you may also add that all those women will also be given the opportunity to choose an evening outfit to wear to a special Colony Ball. He pauses, and then continues:

"After that, you will need first to contact the manager of the Mall and arrange a suitable ballroom date for that event. Then call the manager of the Luxury warehouse and explain that several thousand women will be coming to choose eveningwear outfits suitable for a ball. And finally call the Department of Transport to arrange a series of buses to take the women to the Luxury warehouse to choose their outfits on a series of days well in time for the ball."

Marcus then asks Charlie to join him and Colette at the end of the day when they would take a cab together to Pacific Avenue where he would introduce Charlie to Lorf and see what help the old man could give them.

AFTER THE ULTIMATE VIRUS

The barbecue in the park is a memorable event, with Marcus manning the barbecue, Suyen demonstrating her prowess at turning multiple somersaults on the grass, Charlie doing his tipsy sailor dance routine, and Colette playing some tunes on her trumpet. Then they return to the Pavilion and get stuck into their new work.

Marcus, setting off for his sober Admin office, waves to Colette. "See you this evening, darling," he promises. "You've got your work cut out now!"

Colette then sets off to choose her office in the Pavilion building, carefully selecting a large room with not only a good ocean view, but one with windows that also looked out onto the Esplanade, allowing her to keep an eye on everything that is going on in the area.

Colette, already in hyper-action, leaves her newly-appointed assistant, Melanie, to get on with setting up their office while she goes to her old apartment to use her compudule to get on with the tasks ahead.

"This is the new Colony!" says Colette as she dashes out the door.

That afternoon, Colette works furiously and gets everything done. The TV studio rings immediately asks when the Chief Administrator could be interviewed. Colette checks with Marcus who says that he will do the interview the next day "When my bruise dies down a bit," and he adds: "See you at 5.30. The cab will call at your old apartment to pick you up. Big kisses."

****

Charlie joins them at the gate in the Wire, and Marcus warns him to expect some rough characters in Lorf's gang.

"But you'll find Lorf is a true gentleman," he adds.

The Cleansing Department has cleaned up the blood and guts off the street, and has taken away the two corpses. "I've asked them to give them a decent burial up in the city Domain, with a simple grave sign saying they were members of a gang which launched an assault in Pacific Avenue." Marcus says.

"Fortunately, there aren't any dead bodies from our side."

THE GULLY GROUP GETS GOING

But Marcus speaks too soon. When they enter the building they are met by a silence, broken by occasional grunts and moans and the sound of sobbing.

"What's happened?" asks Marcus, going over to Lorf who is sitting on his decrepit chair, weeping profusely.

"'Aze 'as carked it," he sobs, "'er 'eart was weak from 'er illness and the fight last night knocked 'er out stone cold. Funerals tomorrer...Ma littul wifeys gone..."

"I am so sad to hear that, Lorf," says Marcus, putting his hand on his shoulder. "can Colette and I come to the funeral?"

"Yep," replies Lorf. "Youse is both welcum."

"What time? Asks Marcus.

"3 in aft'noon," says Lorf. "High tide yer see," he adds cryptically.

"Where?" asks Marcus.

"Down at th' Boot," replies Lorf.

"Where's that?" asks Marcus.

"Boot's th' littul deep water bay round corner of th' point," replies Lorf.

"We'll be there," says Marcus. "Now, Lorf, I've brought Charlie to see you. He's going to help us get rid of this gang menace altogether. But we need your help. You know what's going on in gangland and you can tell Charlie what you know about the locations of the gangs and how many there are."

Marcus introduces Charlie to Lorf and leaves the two of them to talk.

Up in the apartment, Marcus embraces Colette. "What a day!" he exclaims. "We achieved a great deal, but my head's aching." He rubs his bruised forehead.

"Come and sit down and I'll get you a cool drink," Colette says, going into the kitchen. "Shall we invite Charlie up for dinner?"

"I think just a drink would suffice," says Marcus, sipping his drink thankfully. "I suspect he might want to get away to see Julie."

"Who's Julie?" Colette inquires.
"She's his long-time partner. I guess they'll be applying for a new joint abode shortly," Marcus replies.

He then tells her about Hazel's death and the funeral the next afternoon. "I've said we'll attend it," he says.

"Of course," says Colette. "We should take some flowers – but I don't know where to find white flowers. I can't just lean over fences and pick them, and anyway, there aren't many flower gardens around the Colony. And we don't have a florist shop. "

"I'll ring Karla tomorrow morning. As you know, she has a lovely garden. She'll give you plenty of flowers." Marcus tells her.

A knock on the door announces Charlie, who is impressed with their apartment. "What a great joint!" he exclaims, looking around the rooms and out through the sliding glass doors with approval. "I wouldn't mind getting an apartment here."

"You'd be most welcome," replies Marcus. "But we don't think it would be fair on Lorf and his gang for too many people to be coming and going through what is their abode downstairs. But one day they will have all passed away. Then you can be the first new resident – and Julie too, if you'd like." Charlie smiles broadly at the thought. Marcus doesn't add that, much as he likes Charlie, he would prefer to keep the building to himself and Colette, for the moment at least.

Charlie remarks that Lorf's inside information about the locations of the gangs will greatly help the Army round them up, and he agrees with Marcus's strategy of inducting them into the Army.

"It's a much more sensible idea than throwing them into gaol, and, anyway, we don't have gaols big enough. In fact, the Colony's one gaol, down at the beach, only has two cells, and they've been empty for years. And we won't put them in leg-irons like they did to the early convicts in the first colony," Charlie says, "But we'll certainly lick them into shape. I'm off now to see Julie. I want you and Colette to come over for drinks soon. And Julie can tell you about her fashion project."

Colette is intrigued to meet this Julie and to learn what Charlie meant by her "fashion projects" and she suggests they pay Charlie and Julie a visit early the following week.

"Peace and quiet, at last!" exclaims Marcus, putting his arms around Colette's waist. "I'll whip up some eggs and we'll have a quick omelette before bed."

THE GULLY GROUP GETS GOING

****

The following morning is hectic for Colette. Her office is starting to function and she and Melanie have hired two reliable staffers from Marcus's Admin Department.

Next, Colette decides to bite the bullet and ring Alistair to invite him to come to her new office. "I'd like you to help me," she tells him. (If he could be separated from Marmeduke, a lot of potential trouble from the Elders might be averted.)

"Why?" he asks in a suspicious tone. "I don't see what earthly use I can be to your lot," he spits, "You've taken over the whole joint like a conquering army, treading on all we held precious."

"You have a great deal of knowledge about the Arts which would be valuable to the Colony," Colette says.

Alistair remains antagonistic, but finally agrees to come and see her the following day.

****

Marcus arrives at Colette's new office at lunchtime. "Nice," he remarks, looking around the room. "You need some pictures on the wall," he suggested.

"No," Colette replies, "the view of the beach is pretty good by itself." They gaze out at the beach. The sea that day is azure– "sea green" – and as flat as the proverbial mill pond. Only ripples, not waves, ruffle the shoreline.

They take a cab up to Karla's house on the Hill and meet her waiting at the gate with a large bunch of white flowers – frangipanis, lilies and even some late-flowering white roses. "I'd invite you both in," Karla says, "But Harold is having his nap and I've got to go to a committee meeting for our bridge club. I must say, I envy you two, being in the thick of things."

Marcus kisses her on the cheek. "Don't you worry, Karla, my dear," he says. "I've got plans for you. As soon as I get through the load of work I've got at the moment, I'll take you to a house we're thinking of making the Colony's official residence. You would be of great assistance with getting the place ready for

business – and helping with the receptions we plan to hold there."
Karla brightens at this and promises to be of help.

She turns to Colette. "My dear, you had Alistair around your little finger at my party. But beware of Marmeduke, he's plotting something. I'll let you know if I find out anything." She then kisses both Colette and Marcus goodbye and they get back into the cab with the flowers and set off for Pacific Avenue and the funeral.

20

CEREMONY AT THE BOOT

JUST BEFORE 3pm, Colette and Marcus, leaning over the balcony railing, hear the sound of a saucepan being beaten rhythmically, and then they see a ragged procession stagger out through the entrance of the garage, carrying the little, misshapen body of Hazel, wrapped tightly in an old blanket, and laid out on a bier fashioned from some of the weapon sticks used in the battle two days earlier.

Colette and Marcus, carrying their flowers, go downstairs and follow the procession, keeping a respectful distance behind it. They round the point and there, before them, is the Boot: a small bay surrounded by looming cliffs and stacks of rocks. The dark green-black sea surges up the rocks and then sucks itself back with a snarling, hissing sound before surging again. A few seagulls hover and squawk, and an occasional fish jumps, silver, out of the swirling water.

The little procession stops, and the mourners put the bier down on a flat rock and stand silently. Colette and Marcus step forward and place some of their flowers on the wrapped body before handing the rest of the flowers to Lorf, who nods his thanks. Then the man with the saucepan begins beating it again and another man, wearing an old red dressing gown tassel around his neck, starts chanting. Colette and Marcus strain their ears, but the strong breeze that is now blowing wafts the words away over the waves. After more chanting, the pall-bearers lift the little body, and, together, heave it with all their strength out and down into the depths below. Lorf throws the rest of the white flowers after the body, and gentle petals float over the dark wind-ruffled water as the body sinks away, deep. Colette feels a tear running down her cheek and she turns to Marcus, who, she observes, is damp-eyed too. Once again, respectfully, they leave the funeral group and walk back to their apartment and go out onto the balcony where the sit in silence for a while.

21

BITTER-SWEET NEWS

COLETTE WAKES up feeling queasy next morning. She goes to her bathroom and throws up, and she doesn't feel like having any breakfast.

"Too much good food lately, I'm not used to it," she explains to Marcus, who has been looking at her with concern.

By the time she reaches her office and prepares for her meeting with Alistair, Colette is feeling her normal self.

Alistair arrives, looking distinctly disgruntled. "I've come out of courtesy, Colette," he says, "But I don't see the point of a meeting."

"Well," says Colette, seating him in an armchair opposite her. "As you know, I am now Head of the Department of Communications & Culture. The Communications side, I can manage easily. But I will need the help of a true expert when it comes to the Cultural activities, and of all the people in the Colony, you stand out as being the most knowledgeable about all aspects of art, music and literature..." Colette pauses to observe Alistair's reaction. *Lay it on with a trowel*, she tells herself. "Indeed, you are the most cultured person in the Colony, and I would like to invite you to join me in raising the Colony's awareness of the high points of culture achieved by the world over the ages, right up to the end of The Best of Times."

Alistair sits forward in his chair, a gleam of interest in his eyes and a self-satisfied smile on his lips. "Yes..." he says. "Go on..."

Colette then outlines some schemes she has thought of to stimulate interest in the Arts throughout the Colony. For example, she suggests, each month an exhibition could be staged up the Mall with artworks brought down from the old Art Gallery in the city...new works of art commissioned...films found in the archives screened...chamber music concerts...new music composed...

"You, Alistair would be our Art Supremo. I will provide suitable staff for you and help with transporting art works down to the Colony. You can give the Colony the benefit of your wonderful knowledge and appreciation of the finer things in life. This Colony may well be the only bastion of human civilisation remaining on the planet. Your contribution would be extremely valuable."

By this time, Alistair is purring.

"My dear Colette," he says, leaning forward again. "I would be delighted to be of service. I knew from the first time we met that you are a woman of integrity and taste. I am happy to be of service to the Department. When shall I begin?"

Colette smiles and leans over and shakes his hand.

"You may start whenever you're ready," she says. "You might like a few days to think and make plans. I'm sure you'll come up with many novel and worthwhile ideas. Remember, we do need to give the Colony some kind of over-all concept of the artistic endeavour over the centuries, from primitive art, through the Egyptian and the Grecian period, the Roman, Persian, Chinese, Indian...Mediaeval...Modern... the Third Reich poster art...right up to the end of The Best of Times when art had reached a dizzy but self-indulgent height.

"And we must cultivate new talent," she continues.

She then stands up and Alistair shakes her hand again and promises to return in a few days with a plan.

****

The next couple of days are packed with activity. The new departments come to life and the Pavilion is a hive of energy and innovation. The Colony is on the move.

"It just shows how much talent and drive was being suppressed under the Elders' control," Marcus comments.

"I guess we'll all have to make sure we don't fall into the traps that pulled down The Best of Times," remarks Colette.

"Yes," Marcus agrees "we're in a very curious stage now. On the one hand, we have a set-up that's like an ideal example of the old Welfare State with free housing, free food, free education, free health care – something the old Socialists would have died for. But just as their Welfare States collapsed financially eventually, going deeper and deeper into debt – so too would ours if we went on for much longer relying on things we have salvaged instead of making our own. And the old Welfare States killed off all spirit of enterprise, leaving a population of zombies, much like the way we were heading. But thank goodness, there's a new energy already starting in the Colony."

Every morning, Colette finds herself feeling ill. She can't face breakfast, and she's beginning to suspect she might be pregnant. Finally, she goes to the pharmacy depot and obtains a pregnancy testing kit. Not surprisingly, it registers "Positive". She is indeed pregnant.

It's little wonder, really, she thinks, *after what Marcus and I have been up to these last months.* And she sighs. On the one hand, she's thrilled to think she's carrying Marcus's child. On the other, she's disturbed by this sudden news. It shocks her out of the dream she's been in since she has fallen in love with Marcus. *It's all too sudden,* she thinks, *we've only started our relationship. Nobody else in the Colony has had a child by someone they know.* Then Colette realises, with a start, that she would, under the strict rules of the Colony, have to undergo an abortion. *How will Marcus react to the news?* she wonders. *He's completely unaware that I was no longer protected by the contraceptive injection. I should have warned him – but I simply couldn't tell him.*

Colette waits until after dinner and they're sitting, as usual, out on the balcony, watching the waves and sipping their drinks.

"Marcus," she begins. "I have something serious, very serious, to tell you."

"Oh!" says Marcus. "What? I'm all ears."

She takes a deep breath. "Marcus. I'm pregnant."

Marcus turns to her in surprise, then a look of intense joy comes over his face.

"But, darling, that's wonderful news!" he exclaims, reaching for her hand. "I'm a bit surprised, because I thought you were covered by the injection, like all the women in the Colony, but it's fabulous news. Just think of it, our own baby!"

Colette begins to sob quietly. "But, Marcus, I'm not allowed to have a baby. It's the rule of the Colony. I have to undergo the pregnancy program like everyone else. I'm going to have to have an abortion."

Marcus takes her in his arms. "No, no, no," he's almost shouting. "No way will we lose our baby! Let me think what we can do."

Colette continues to sob. Her whole world seems to be in tatters. How foolish she's been not to tell Marcus she'd been taken off the injection.

Finally, he sits up straight and says: "I have the answer. As you know, my clone sister, Annie, is the head of the Infirmary. We'll go and tell her what has happened and swear her to secrecy. Then we'll ask her to have you go through the pregnancy program like everyone else, but you won't have an abortion, nor will you undergo artificial insemination. Then you'll have the baby – our baby.. – just like all the other women. Nobody needs to know the truth."

Colette brightens at this, but then she points out the pitfalls to this plan.

"First of all, I would be giving birth earlier than the timing of the program, and I wouldn't be able to claim the baby as my very own – our very own. I'd have to give it up to the Nannies, like all the other women. And," she adds, "It's deceitful to trick everyone, and it's unfair on the other women in the program. I don't know what we can do."

Marcus then says that another idea is forming in his mind. "I guess I never really thought about all this before I met you, Colette," he begins. "Like the other men in the Colony, I didn't have much of a clue about what the women had to undergo. Karla was past the call-up dates for the pregnancy by the time I met her. And, until now, I didn't realise the pitfall of a woman getting pregnant outside the program.

"I think it's time for a major change in policy. Yes, we will have to continue with the pregnancy program for a year or so, to ensure we reach our population goal. The program has been very effective in producing strong, healthy children for the Colony. But it does reek of sinister eugenics, too, like the ideas the Nazis promulgated."

BITTER-SWEET NEWS

He goes on to outline his plan: the pregnancy program should be changed to permit couples who can prove they really love and care about each other and have established a permanent relationship, to have their own babies. They would still go through parts of the program to ensure reaching the population target. They'd need to start on the ovulation pills at the age of 23, and so on. But they could have their own child, or children.

"We'll go and see Annie tomorrow," he says. "And we'll make an announcement about the change in the pregnancy program rule shortly. It will work well with the new re-housing policy too. But I think the role of the Nannies shouldn't be scrapped. They do an excellent job and they should still be in charge of the babies during weekdays because we need the women back at work as soon as possible after the births. But a couple will be able to see their baby after work hours and they can take it home at weekends."

Colette looks at Marcus. "That's wonderful, Marcus," she cries, "I think you've solved our problem. We can have our own baby and we won't have cheated on the Colony. And many other women will be very pleased too."

They lie together for a while, absorbing the momentous decision, then Marcus rests his head between her legs, starting to kiss her. Colette's body arches and convulses in response. "Marcus…," she moans with pleasure.

"Now it's your turn, Colette," says Marcus rolling over on to his back, and Colette goes down on him.

They lie together for a while longer and then come together in a final climax.

Marcus puts his hand on her stomach. "I think I'm going to enjoy your pregnancy," he says, smiling.

Probably more than I will, she thinks.

****

Next morning they call in to the Infirmary and go into Annie's office. Colette is curious to meet Marcus's sister. She immediately sees the similarities: they both have the same dark, almost black, hair, although Annie's is curlier. And Annie has the same hazel-brown eyes flecked with gold. Annie is pleased to

141

finally meet Colette in the flesh. Marcus explains why they have come to see her, and Annie looks thoughtful.

"Marcus and Colette," she finally says. "I agree. It is time the program began to be changed. It has worried me for some time, but my hands were tied by the grip the Elders had on the community.

"I'm very glad to meet you at last, Colette. Marcus has told me lots about you. And congratulations to both of you about the baby – my future niece or nephew! If you make the announcement of the new plan soon, Marcus, I'll set the wheels of change in motion here.

"Meanwhile, Colette, you'd better undergo the usual medical checks, but from the look of you, you're in blooming good health."

They get up to go, and Annie holds out her hand to Colette. "I'd like to get to know you more soon. How about we ask Marcus to give us lunch one day soon at his yellow house?"

****

Marcus makes the big announcement about the changes to the pregnancy program on TV on New Year's Day and the reaction from the Colony is virtually unanimous.

"About bloody time," is a typical comment; it would seem the Colony is rapidly embracing the humanising of its world.

With the problem of her pregnancy now solved, Colette is able to throw herself into her work as head of the Department of Communication & Culture. Alistair proves as good as his word, coming up with an imaginative program to foster interest in the Arts. He seems completely reconciled to now being part of the new regime, much to Marmeduke's dismay.

Marmeduke, too, has been busy – plotting a reverse takeover of the Colony with his other Elders. But now that Alistair has defected, Marmeduke begins to realise his cause is lost.

A few days later, Marmeduke is found dead, sprawled out on the rocks at the north point of the beach. He apparently committed suicide early in the morning."

"Oh!" says Colette. "I don't really know what to say. I must admit I'm not sorry."

BITTER-SWEET NEWS

"Me either," says Marcus, and they don't discuss the matter further.

****

Colette and Marcus go over to Charlie's apartment for drinks later in the week. Colette is curious to meet Julie and wonders why they hadn't met before. *She must work in some out-of-the-way department*, Colette thinks, as they wait for Charlie to come to the door. He ushers them into his little living-room, offering them drinks and calling out to Julie: "They've arrived!"

Julie then enters the room, an extraordinary sight, which leaves Colette momentarily speechless. She is over six feet tall, with green hair to match piercing green eyes. She is wearing a retro-punk outfit with thigh-high black leather boots and her arms are festooned with bangles. "Hi Colette and Marcus," she says in a lilting voice. "I've been dying to meet you both. Charlie tells me about the amazing things you're doing and of course I saw you, Colette, on TV with your Elephant Walk. That was too super for words," she says, using retro-slang to match her outfit.

Colette is intrigued by Julie. She hasn't imagined Charlie's girlfriend would be so zany – she'd thought Charlie would have chosen some quiet mouse of a girl who was a foil for his flamboyant personality. But no – Julie is a really dominating figure. As they sit chatting, Colette finds herself warming to her. It turns out Julie works in the Luxury warehouse as an assistant manager.

"I'm not eligible on my Grade 2 to go to the Luxury warehouse, so it's no wonder I've never met you before," Colette remarks.

"It's great working there," Julie says, her bangles jangling. "I get all kinds of perks – like green hair dye, and lots of smashing clothes to try out." There's something refreshing about Julie's down-to-earth, matter-of-fact manner and the way she cuts through formalities and brings a fresh perspective to what is being discussed. By the end of their drinks session, Colette finds herself offering her a fashion column to write for the Colony newspaper. "Our new little paper is very serious," Colette explains. "We're covering all the reforms that are starting in the Colony, and so on,

143

but it needs brightening up a bit. A spunky fashion column – for both the girls and the boys – would bring a bit of frivolity and humour to the pages."

"I'd love to do it," Julie says, "But it would ruin my plans. I always aim to stay ahead of the latest trends. If I wrote about what I'm wearing, everyone would start wearing what I'm wearing."

"But you don't have to write about your very latest fashion craze," Colette pleads, "You could simply write about the craze you've just grown out of. Then, while everyone's starting to dye their hair green, for example, and to wear retro punk you could be donning pastels or whatever…"

"OK," Julie says, shaking Colette's hand. "It's a deal. When do you want me to start?"

"Could you come into my office one day next week with your first column?" Colette asks, and Julie agrees.

On their way home, Colette remarks to Marcus that Julie seems a really interesting girl.

"Well, 'girl' isn't exactly the right word for Julie," Marcus says. "Because, actually… Julie's a bloke."

"Oh!" exclaims Colette, taken aback. "Oh, well, I like her no matter what."

****

Over the next month, the Gully Group heads of new departments work fast and furiously on their plans. At a meeting about a month after the election, they make their reports. Phil, as head of Housing Re-location, announces that the first new accommodation would be ready by the end of February

Alice reports she is making slow, but steady progress with framing a new Constitution.

"Good," says Marcus. "Alice, just keep working on it. Remember it's likely we shan't see a Constitution being necessary for a good while, but we need to get thinking about it now, so that when the new country is ready to take that leap, there's a sensible document for the experts to work on.

"Back in the Best of Times, Australians still swore allegiance to the British Crown. We need to cope with the fact that our links to Great Britain, tenuous though they were during The Best of

Times, are now totally defunct. It doesn't look as if there's anyone left in Great Britain, let alone a King or Queen to swear allegiance to. A republic is definitely the way to go."

On the Grand Ball front, Colette reports that already many busloads of women have travelled to the luxury depot to choose their reward of eveningwear. "But there are still many hundreds more," she says. "We're going to have to scour the little boutiques out in the suburbs if we want to satisfy the full demand."

She adds that all is going well in the Communications area. The Colony newspaper will go out online shortly.

Rodney's sport and recreation onslaught is progressing too. "Going great guns," is how he puts it.

Simon reports that quite a few people who work in the bureaucracy have expressed a desire to take up farming, and they are being assessed and given experience on his farm and at the one out near the Mountains to test their response to the real thing.

Charlie says his Army is starting to develop a putative Navy. "We've found some pretty large, strong yachts moored around the Harbour," he reports, "And quite a few Army lads and lasses are trying their hands at sailing. I know we don't need a Navy at the moment, but one would come in handy if we wanted to sail round the continent to see if there's anyone still alive around the place. Little does he realise how important a naval presence will soon be.

Finally, William reports that the spy network has been dismantled. "We've found some pretty suspicious, nasty stuff in it," he says. "It'll help you to sort out who you can trust and who you can't in the Department of Admin."

Next, William continues, his Department is looking into how to improve the partially-disabled Internet. "That's our next big thing," he concludes. "Even if there's no-one out there to communicate with, we can use the repaired Internet to try and dig into all kinds of data that's been inaccessible – as you already know, Colette."

With everything progressing well, Marcus feels it's a good time to make some trips to the country areas to discuss progress and problems with the Regional Heads. That evening, he asks Colette if she'd like to accompany him to some of the outlying areas.

"I've now got Jim and Sophie's old car fixed," he says, "It is very strong – and much smoother on bumpy roads. Would you like to learn how to drive it? Oh, and by the way, I've now got that trunk of papers you found down in the garage. We can have a look at them when we get back."

Colette agrees to the travel plan and they decide to set off two days later. She's eager, but slightly fearful of what it would be like on the open road, out in the wild countryside. The farthest she's ever travelled outside the Wire is on an occasional visit into the old, gated city, on Department business.

"Don't worry, Colette," says Marcus, noticing her concern. "I'll look after you – and there aren't any wild beats, just kangaroos, koalas and wallabies. It was far more dangerous that day we ventured down to the garage under our building. Thankfully, Charlie got his Army boys to clean the place out.

"What happened to the dogs?" Colette asks.

"They shot them," replies Marcus curtly, "they were an absolute menace."

22

THE GRAND BALLS

INVIGORATED AND INSPIRED by the trip down south, Colette throws herself into the production of the online newspaper, and the organisation of the Grand Balls. (After totting up the numbers, she has decided the only way to cope with so many attendees is to hold a series of Balls). The Balls will take place in the Mall ballroom in March.

By mid-February, Colette is about three months' pregnant, and Marcus is enjoying her slowly-growing voluptuousness. "Don't worry about getting a bit plumper while you're pregnant, it suits you to have a little bit more weight – though I look forward to your old slim figure," he adds hastily, as he watches her getting dressed ready to go to the Infirmary for her first check-up.

At the Infirmary, Annie greets her. "We're going to give you a scan," she says. "That'll give us some idea of exactly how pregnant you are. It will be useful to have a precise date for when you're due." The Infirmary is quite well-equipped with surgical equipment salvaged from the big hospitals in the city, and Colette is given a gown and told to lie down ready for the scan.

After it's over, the nurse comes up with a big smile: "Congratulations, Colette. Your twins are looking fine and healthy. They are a boy and a girl."

Twins! Colette sits up in surprise. She has been imagining, all this time, a single baby. She can hardly wait to tell Marcus.

Back home at Pacific Avenue that evening, they lie in bed, discussing possible names for the pair.

"I'd like Rose for our daughter," Marcus finally decides. "I don't know why, but it's a nice name."

"And I'd like to call our son, Rory," says Colette, much to her own surprise.

Marcus laughs, "OK!" he agrees. "It does have a certain ring to it!"

AFTER THE ULTIMATE VIRUS

****

Colette soon realises the enormity of what she has entered into with the organisation of the Grand Balls. There are far more women eligible to attend the Ball – and thus eligible for an evening dress – than she had envisaged. She has done her sums and has counted up a rough total of 36,000 women who have undergone the pregnancy program between the year 2045 when the First (faulty) Cloning had begun, through to 2080 when cloning ended and Artificial Insemination started, and then on up to the present day. Added to that is the relative handful of women who had undergone Invitro treatment in the early days before cloning, and Colette tots up a final total of 42,000 evening dresses that have to be provided as part of the reward promised by the Colony to the women.

Oh my god! Colette gasps when she looks at the figures. *Finding all that evening gear's going to be an uphill job. Still, looking on the bright side, it means the population of the colony more than doubled over that period – especially taking into account the large number of twins resulting from the ovulation pills the women – like me – took.*

It is about time a proper census of the Colony is undertaken, she decides.

Eveningwear search parties are sent out, not only to the central luxury warehouse, but also into the darkest reaches of the outer suburbs where tiny long closed down boutiques are plundered for suitable outfits for the Colony's heroines.

Inevitably, stressful incidents occur – like the time Maureen 830 grabs a red taffeta dress from the warehouse display rail just as Carlotta 640 is reaching for it. The two women tear at one another and Maureen pulls out a hunk of Carlotta's hair, announcing triumphantly that she's suspected it was a wig all along.

Colette then books the Mall ballroom every night for two months, packing in the guests and their partners according to their ages and which clone batches they belong to. Buses are arranged, a couple of bands are booked, a menu chosen, decorations found in the luxury depot, and, after further couture dramas, the fun begins. The women thoroughly enjoy the limelight and being recognised for their sacrifice, and the Colony's blokes manage to deck themselves out in reasonably suitable clothing to match their partners' finery.

Colette and Marcus attend one Ball a week for the first month, but her pregnancy – by May she is reaching the sixth month mark – gives her a good excuse to refrain from indulging in the old-style dances like the waltz and the foxtrot any further. Melanie, herself now also pregnant – to Rodney – takes over the role of Ball hostess, because she is only at the two-months stage. Rodney happily escorts her throughout the May Balls; he's fully committed to her and they have been allocated a little terrace house not far from the beach, and quite close to a terrace house Marcus and Colette have found for when their babies arrive, because a nursery would be necessary for the babies' weekend visits.

Meanwhile, Colette and Marcus continue to split their existence between Number 2, Pacific Avenue during the working week, and the yellow Gully House at weekends. They find it an ideal arrangement, and life is both fulfilling and enjoyable.

"You know, Colette," Marcus says one evening when they are sitting up in bed, leaning against their piled-up pillows. "The world has taken on a completely new dimension since we met."

"Totally," Colette agrees dreamily as she nuzzles into Marcus's shoulder. "It has been a bit like waking up on a new planet. I love you dearly."

It is starting to get colder now, with winter just around the corner. Marcus finds some electric heaters for their apartment at Pacific Avenue, and he readies the grates at the Gully House for wood fires. He also arranges regular deliveries of kindling wood for Lorf and his gang. None of them are getting any younger and Marcus has watched them struggling up from the point, carrying meagre supplies of driftwood from the beach.

The Colony itself, too, is enjoying life. Suyen and Harold have worked hard to get a market economy happening and already a couple of little cafes, operated by former bureaucrats from the Department of Administration, have erected striped awnings and put chairs and tables out on the pavement, immediately attracting delighted Colonists, who are learning how to augment their employment grade allowances with real money for the first time in their lives. Other little shops are starting up too. One business in particular is flourishing, – a repair shop. Their industrious owner and his partner, formerly employed in the Colony kitchen, now mend shoes, darn socks, sew on buttons and shorten hems on clothing which, in The Best of Times, would have been thrown out after one or two wears. Another shop that's thriving is a pottery studio, initiated by Alice, run by two busy young potters who have found a clay deposit not far from the old golf course and have set up a kiln and are churning out hand-made crockery, painted with original beach designs, to sell to Colonists tired of the regulation plastic tableware.

Simon has recruited quite an army of trainee farmers and has deployed some of them into repairing the ancient water reservoir near the city park, and cleaning-out and reconnecting the old water pipes. The growing Colony now has a reliable water supply and no longer needs to rely solely on rainwater tanks.

Meanwhile, Charlie and the Army have inspected the condition of the great highway which stretches west over the Mountains, and, to their relief, have found that most of it, apart from stretches where boulders have fallen onto the roadway, is in fairly reasonable condition. This has allowed them to speed up reaching the disabled astro-radio-telescope centre out on the western plains on the other side of the Mountains.

Marcus makes several expeditions over the Mountains to the astro-radio-telescope centre, promising Colette that he'll take her for a trip to the Mountains once she's had the twins. "And we can see if we can find Jim and Sophie's little house up there too," he promises, "You know, the one where Sophie went to live after Jim was killed."

This idea particularly pleases Colette, who is by now in her eighth month and working from home and getting the nursery ready for the twins, whose kicking and shoving are starting to make life quite uncomfortable for her as her belly swells. She's finding the waiting tedious and decides to open the trunk she'd found in the garage when Marcus was inspecting the car. The moment she opens the trunk, Colette, sees it's full of old press cuttings from Sophie's early days as a journalist, before newspapers stopped production. Opening a scrapbook compiled by a very young Sophie, obviously exceedingly proud of her efforts, Colette comes across a story and photo that jolts her. Sophie had scrawled at the top of the cutting: "My very first story in print!" Under the somewhat prosaic heading: GATEHOUSE OPENED Colette reads a story, by-lined Sophie Seagrem, about the official opening by the Mayor of a gatehouse at the entrance to the park where the football stadium still is – not far from the Council Chambers.

****

Finally, Colette goes into labour. Marcus takes her to the Infirmary where Annie greets her and takes her to the maternity ward. Marcus asks her if she wants him to come into the ward with her, but Colette decides Marcus can wait outside But before he goes outside, a nurse comes up to him: "Sir," she says. "I need to take a tiny piece of tissue for your DNA record. All the parents – both the mothers and the fathers – of children born in the Colony must have their DNA checked. Usually, this occurs before the start of a pregnancy, because, until now, the fathers are sperm donors and their DNA is checked for compatibility with the mother. But you, sir, are our first natural father!" Marcus complies with her request and then gives Colette a hug before leaving.

The pain is agonising, but thankfully reasonably brief, and soon Colette is sitting up in bed, a twin on either arm, with Marcus back, looking relieved and proud, sitting beside her. Rose has a fluff of strawberry-blond hair and what looked like being hazel-brown eyes, just like Marcus's, while Rory has a shock of almost black hair, just like his father's, and what would be deep blue eyes, like Colette's. Marcus is overwhelmed by it all. "I still can't believe I'm a father," he says. "We're parents, oh my god! We must do everything in our power to make our world good for them."

Colette obediently follows the Infirmary protocol, leaving her babies behind in the Creche in the care of their Nanny, but visiting them every afternoon until the weekends when she and Marcus pick them up and take them to the terrace house with its nursery. She and Marcus struggle at first to cope with two yowling babies, but things settle down into a happy nappy routine (we shan't dwell further on this period of their domestic life.)

About six weeks after the birth of the twins, Marcus asks Colette if she feels like taking a trip up the Mountains, to which she agrees with alacrity. "It would certainly do me some good," she says, poking he head through a washing line of nappies in the back garden. And it will be a little holiday before I go back to work again."

It is now late August and spring is in the air as they drive towards the Mountains. "They aren't very high," remarks Colette as she looks at the mountain range ahead as they cross the great flat plain which had once been the bed of an enormous river flowing down from mountain peaks, which, millions of years before, had been four time higher than today.

"They get a bit higher as we go," says Marcus. "By the time we reach the top of the range, where Sophie lived, it will be 1065 metres" As they drive they see the wattle has started to come out across the bush, its pale gold adding highlights to the grey-green of the eucalypts. In the distance, the mountains look blue, a hazy mauve-blue caused by eucalyptus oil essence floating in the air above them. The highway winds gradually up hill and down valley for several hours and they pass great swathes of bushland which has been devastated by bushfires in previous years, their blackened trunks and limbs now spouting vivid green leaves once more. "A lot of these trees need fire to regenerate them – the fire makes their seeds open," Marcus says. "It's rather like the way the human race goes through disasters but somehow regenerates itself." The trip to the top of the range used to take an hour-and-a-half back in The Best of Times, when driverless electric cars threaded their way swiftly and seamlessly through the traffic. But now it has taken almost three hours because of the bumpy patches on the roadway, plus areas where rock falls are still being cleared, and they have only reached three quarters of the journey. They stop for lunch at a small, makeshift café-cum-car battery recharging station set up by the Army when they began mending the road. Somewhat refreshed, Marcus and Colette drive on, up-and-up. They pass a lovely old stone church which must have dated back to early colonial days, around 1820, and they see flocks of white cockatoos circling, squawking, above them,

THE GRAND BALLS

An hour or so later, the sun is beginning to dip in the west and Colette is thankful to see a small light glowing at the door of a little inn just ahead of them.

"It's now open because of the workers coming and going from the Colony to the astro-radio-telescope station," Marcus explains. "This is where we stay the night." Inside, a log fire is burning in a cosy sitting- room with comfortable armchairs draped with knitted rugs, and walls hung with old paintings of bush scenes. The landlady greets them and helps them upstairs with their bags, where they find an old brass bed with its sheets turned down, waiting for them after they have their dinner of roast lamb, peas and carrots, followed by custard and apple pie.

"This is the first time I've enjoyed myself completely for months," laughs Colette, throwing off her clothes and jumping, naked, into the bed. Marcus sits on the bed for a moment, gazing at her lithe, once-more-slim, body.

"Welcome back, the old, lovely, darling Colette," he almost groans. "Much as I've enjoyed the plumper you, I've been missing the real you dreadfully." And they make love passionately before falling into a deep mountain-air sleep, clinging to one another.

Next morning, they go in search of the house where Sophie had fled just before the Calamity and where she had ended her days. From her diary, they have learned that her house had been situated towards the end of a long road leading off the big highway. Now they are driving through what used to be a happy little township, with its stores and cafes, which had obviously attracted the tourist trade, but had also been home to many well-heeled retirees and younger families, But now it is completely deserted. They reach the little street where Sophie's house still is – perched above a vast forest of gumtrees, stretching far to the horizon. A few magpies warble and the odd kookaburra guffaws into the clear mountain air. The houses in the street resemble a frontier town Colette has seen in the movies

They find Sophie's house and negotiate a flight of wooden stairs, looking down into a tangled garden filled with plants that have grown, uncontrolled, for over 60 years. Colette can identify, from her botany classes at school, that there are bottlebrush trees (*Callistemon*) and fuchsias among the overgrown foliage. The front door has been locked with a strong chain and padlock, by whom? Marcus, thinking ahead as usual, has brought some tools with him and is able to break into the house quite quickly.

"I feel like a burglar," remarks Colette as she makes her way along a glassed-in verandah and into the main upstairs room which still has some Persian rugs on the floor, and bookcases holding rows of books and porcelain ornaments. In one cobwebby room is a computer which had been modern back in 2030. Colette and Marcus open it to see if they can extract a hard drive, but the inside of the CPU is empty. Indeed, they can find no records of Sophie's time in the house. Perhaps she had become ill and someone had helped her take what she was writing with her to a hospital or nursing home? Downstairs is a large room with floor-to-ceiling windows and doors looking out onto the bush. The room contains a large dining table and the kitchen is enormous. Marcus moves instinctively towards the stove, "A gas stove!" he exclaims. "Jim and Sophie must have had marvellous parties up here."

"Well, I guess Jim would have done the cooking," remarks Colette.

"While Sophie entertained the guests!" laughs Marcus. "Come on Colette," he urges, moving to go back upstairs. "I don't feel right intruding into their house like this. Let's go."

"I just need to dig up a lavender plant to take home to the Colony," Colette says, picking up a trowel she has found on the veranda. "I don't know why, but I know exactly where to find the lavender – over there in the corner, past the fishpond." She pushes her way through the tangled undergrowth of what had once been Sophie's garden. "Ah!" she calls out triumphantly. "Here it is!" and she emerges holding a clump of lavender. "I think Sophie's DNA told me where to find it."

They lock up the house securely, promising to come again when the children are old enough.

"Perhaps by then there'll be some other people living back here," Colette says wistfully. "It would be a good place for holidays."

Before leaving the town, they travel down another long road, driving slowly to avoid the potholes and dead trees that had fallen across it in winter storms, and they reach a lookout which Marcus has read about when he was at school.

THE GRAND BALLS

"It's called Govett's Leap," he explains. "it wasn't called that because people leaped off it, although a famous archaeologist, called Vere Gordon Childe, did, but because a 'leap' is an old word from Scotland, meaning 'waterfall' – and there's the waterfall."

Colette chimes in: "I did some research on this place too, before we came. And this is the place where Charles Darwin travelled by horse and coach back in 1836 when he visited this country. He looked out at these mountain ridges with their rocks marked with millions of years of layers of sediment created by fallen gum leaves and mud, and striations caused by shifting rocks, maybe even volcanoes, and his Theory of Evolution was born."

They gaze across the endless mountains before them, covered in thick eucalypts, the blue haze rising from them. "I remember hearing about the early explorers, too," Colette says. "Blaxland, Lawson and Wentworth, and the others. Imagine trying to cross these mountains on foot!"

Silently, they then turn back to the car and set off to the last town at the top of the mountains and start travelling down a sudden, steep, road which winds down towards the western plains, stretching ahead. They remain silent, overwhelmed by the size of the country their little Colony belongs to.

Finally they reach the astro-radio-telescope which is slowly coming back to life with the aid of the growing number of solar panels being set up by Charlie and his Army. The officer in charge greets them and shows them around the facility which used to send out and receive messages from the crews of space expeditions to Mars. "Today, it picks up nothing but static," the officer tells them. But," the officer pauses, "We did pick up a radio message yesterday. Our first. But it's not from outer space. It's from northern Queensland. I haven't reported this yet to anyone because I knew you were coming today."

"What!" exclaims Marcus. "We didn't think anyone was alive up there!"

"The messages seem to be coming from a very small community of people way up north at the tip of the continent. They are tapping out SOS messages and the occasional bit of garbled words which we are not able to identify too clearly. But it seems they are calling for help. we can't seem to be able to contact them – we've tried everything. When you get back to the Colony you might see if one of your technical wizzkids can contact them."

Excited, Marcus replies that as soon as he gets back to the Colony, he'll discuss the news with Charlie and see if the Army might be able to contact them, or if not, they could send out an expedition to find these people.

"We must go to those people's assistance," vows Marcus. "As soon as we get back, I'll start organising a rescue party. We must offer help to anyone in trouble – there are still so very few of us humans left on earth."

23

S.O.S. FROM THE FAR NORTH

BACK HOME in the Colony, Colette feels a sudden rush of maternal warmth for her twins. Picking each little bundle up, and looking into their eyes, she feels she's at last communicating with them. They are now two months old. and she almost, but not quite, feels a pang about leaving them in their Nanny's care when she goes back to work.

No, in the long run, it will be good for them to have a mother who isn't solely devoted to them, she decides. *In this strange new world we're in, they will need to grow up able to stand on their own feet and be independent. But Marcus and I'll always be there for them*

Colette is glad to start work again, especially in the revitalised atmosphere of the Colony. She and Alistair are making progress with the cultural program, and the TV station has given her a weekly spot, as promised, for an Arts program. After work each day, she and Marcus go to see the twins and give them their bottles before they are tucked up for the night. At weekends they take the twins home with them, either to the Gully House or to the terrace house. Pacific Avenue, with Lorf's crowd at the entrance, is a little difficult for transporting young babies and their paraphernalia.

Marcus, meanwhile, is helping Charlie and the Colony's tiny Navy prepare themselves for a long sea voyage up to the very north of the continent in their rescue mission to the people up there who are still sending SOS messages. Every morning before going into his office, Marcus joins Charlie for sea trials on the harbour and then out into the ocean on board the SS *Sophie*, as Marcus has dubbed her, much to Colette's delight. A 48-foot, sturdy yacht which the Army has salvaged from its harbour mooring, the *Sophie* is made mainly of fibreglass and is in good condition for her age, with very few parts vulnerable to rust. She can happily

157

carry a crew of eight, and there is room for a few passengers – if the people calling for help need to be taken back to the Colony. Marcus finds sailing exhilarating, trimming the sails to catch every gust of wind, tacking across the deep green water as gulls whirl above the sails.

I'm the happiest man alive! he thinks one golden morning as he holds the tiller of the *Sophie* and the wind billows the sails.

By the first week in November the *Sophie* and her crew are ready to sail off north, when disaster strikes. Charlie has been out that morning on a training trip into rugged bushland with the crew, getting them ready to tackle whatever terrain they might encounter when they reach land up north. Climbing up a steep sandstone cliff, Charlie's foot dislodges a stone which then dislodges another stone, and soon half the cliff-face comes tumbling down, with Charlie falling, heavily, down to the bottom, issuing a string of expletives, followed by heavy groans. "I'm fucked," he groans. "Must've broken something." The crew carry him to their truck and rush him back to the Colony where he is transported by the Colony ambulance to the Infirmary where he's diagnosed with a badly-fractured leg which requires an operation.

Marcus and Colette visit him that afternoon and find a very sorry-looking Charlie sitting up in his hospital bed. "Marcus," he says, "What are we going to do? I won't be able to sail for a couple of weeks…"

"More like a month or two," Marcus interrupts him, "We can't leave those people up there that long. I'll take over command of the *Sophie* – I know how to sail her now."

"Could you?" asks Charlie, brightening for a moment, "But you have important business down here. The Colony can't do without you."

"No, "Marcus replies. "I wouldn't be away long – just a couple of weeks. I'd be back by Christmas. It'll do me good to get away from my desk for a while. It'll clear my mind."

And so it is decided, much to Colette's dismay, that Marcus will take over the rescue expedition up north.

Marcus and Colette go home to Pacific Avenue that evening after visiting the twins, and sit out on the balcony, somewhat stunned by the turn of events. "I won't be away long, Colette, darling," Marcus sooths her. "You'll be busy enough getting your

Department back in order after your absence. And Rose and Rory need you."

Charlie, now convalescing in Julie's care, warns Marcus that it is the beginning of the cyclone season. "Be careful and sail close to shore if the weather looks bad," he advises. "And wear your life jacket." Marcus is a little surprised, but touched nonetheless, that Charlie cares for his safety.

The next few days are busy with preparations for the voyage. Marcus tells Lorf he will be away at sea for a while and asks him to keep an eye on their apartment while he's away. "Colette will be staying in the terrace house down in the Colony, with the twins," he explains.

"'Ave a safe voyge," Lorf says, looking concerned.

On the eve of the voyage, Marcus and Colette go to see the twins on the way home.

"Goodbye, my darlings," Marcus says, giving both babies a cuddle. "Look after your mother while I'm away." A gurgle or two in response perhaps signifies goodbye.

That evening after dinner, Colette and Marcus sit on the balcony and gaze out over the ocean, silently conjuring up images of Marcus's voyage ahead.

"I'll miss you dreadfully while you're away," sighs Colette, leaning over and holding his hand.

"I'll be in wireless contact with you all the way, and some of the satellites are back in service now, too, and I shan't be away long. Let's go inside now," suggests Marcus, leading her into the bedroom. "I want to make love to every bit of you, so I can think about tonight while I'm away."

They make love tenderly and then fall into a dep slumber until the early hours when Colette awakes suddenly, sitting up in the bed.

"Don't go, Jim!" she screams. "Don't go!"

Marcus awakes, startled by her scream.

"You called me 'Jim'," he says. "You must have been having a dream."

"It was a nightmare," sobs Colette, clinging to him. "I could suddenly feel exactly how Sophie felt when she heard the news that Jim had been killed. I felt it right through my whole body, through my arms, my legs…"

"Calm down, Colette, my darling," Marcus sooths her. "All will be well, and I'll be back by Christmas. It'll do me good to get out of the office for a while. This desk job gets me down sometimes. I'll miss you dreadfully while I'm away, but I'll be back soon. Remember, history never repeats itself."

Comforted, Colette goes back to sleep, while Marcus gets up for a while and stands, leaning over the balcony railing, contemplating the heaving sea below.

The *Sophie* sets sail next morning, or at least, it starts its fuel engine briefly while it manoeuvres out from the wharf. The sails will be unfurled and hoisted shortly because motor fuel is very scarce.

Colette stands on the wharf, waving to Marcus and the crew. He blows a kiss to her as *Sophie* slides out into the harbour. Colette feels tears streaming down her cheeks and she turns away and stumbles back to the roadway where her taxi is waiting. She tells it to take her to the staff canteen where she has a cup of coffee. Rodney comes in and sits down next to her. "Colette," he says in a sympathetic tone. "I know how you must be feeling. Just know that I can be called on at any time if you need help. Melanie and I would like to invite you to dinner this evening. Our son, Tim, is almost old enough to play with your two."

Colette thanks him and agrees to join him and Melanie for dinner. She doesn't know how she's going to get through the empty nights. Then, being Colette, she throws herself into her work, sorting out problems that have mounted during her last month of pregnancy and the time afterwards when she stayed at home. Everyone in her department rallies round and tries to take her mind off the voyage.

After work, she goes to see the twins and helps their Nanny feed them and change their nappies. *Doing this helps to keep my mind off things*, she thinks.

Next evening, Colette receives her first message from Marcus: **"All going well. Sea calm. Crew settling in. I miss you, my darling. Take care, love and kisses to you and the babes, M."** Colette's mind flies back to the first time Marcus had contacted her, when he indicated in his secret note that he wanted to accompany her to Pacific Avenue and had signed the note 'M'. *So much has happened since then!* she muses. *So very, very much.*

S.O.S. FROM THE FAR NORTH

The week passes slowly for Colette as she goes through her daily routine, functioning efficiently but with only half her mind on what she's doing. Marcus sends daily reports. The wind has blown from the south most of the way, pushing *Sophie* along fast. They had passed by some islands one day. **"Their white sand looked so inviting,"** he radios. **"I felt like pulling in, dropping anchor, and taking a swim, like I do every day at Bondi."**

Finally, *Sophie* and her captain and crew reach the northern tip of the continent and locate the beleaguered little group of settlers who had sent the SOS. **"We had to hack our way through dense jungle to get to them,"** Marcus radios. **"We still had our sea legs, which made it difficult to move quickly. But we found them -15 men and women and a couple of children. They were in a pitiful state due to malaria. Some of their number had died, and the rest were so weak they weren't able to find enough food to live on. They are the descendants of a group of missionaries stranded up there when the Calamity happened and they have no idea of what has happened in the world since The Calamity. One of them recently found an old wireless set and fiddled with it till it started to work, which is how they contacted us. Because their radio equipment is so old and faulty, they could only transmit, not receive. Anyway, we offered to take some of them back to the Colony and they thankfully accepted. They'll leave behind the ones who have more-or-less recovered from the malaria because they like living there. We hope to be able to fit the ill ones into *Sophie* alright."**

Colette is thankful to learn they'd finally made dry land and are on the point of return. Christmas with Marcus back home is all she can think of now.

The following evening, she hears from Marcus again.

"Out at sea, homeward bound. Seas rough and winds high. All my love, missing you. M."

That is the last time she hears from Marcus. One of Charlie's Navy officers contacts Colette "There's a very big cyclone heading towards the *Sophie*," he warns her. "I'll keep you informed."

161

24

THE WINTER OF DESPAIR

BESIDE HERSELF with worry, Colette returns to her office and sits numbly at her desk, her hands clenched. Everyone tries to comfort her, but to no avail. The Navy officer reports the following day, telling her the cyclone is a vicious one, causing havoc as it travels down the coast.

A week goes by, and still no contact from Marcus. Charlie, now back on duty, but still in plaster, deploys a second Navy yacht to set off to the rescue; obviously *Sophie* is in trouble.

She's a tough boat," soothes Charlie, "They're probably anchored in some cove until the storm departs. Their radio contact has been cut off by the storm. We'll find them before too long and get them back safe and sound, even if we have to tow them the whole way."

Colette's fears are abated a little by Charlie's reassurance, but she can barely concentrate on her work.

The days drift by and still no word from Marcus. The reconnaissance boat scours the Queensland coastline and nearby islands to no avail.

Two months pass, and still no word. The Navy yacht finally gives up the search. Their aquadrones have raked over the whole area of ocean where the *Sophie* had charted her course. Nothing could be found of the yacht, not a skerrick of her has washed up on the mainland sand. The jungle and bushland for kilometres inland were scoured by landrones. There are no islands within a thousand square kilometres of where the crew had last been in contact. The *Sophie* has sunk without trace, is the verdict.

Finally, the navy boat returns to the Colony and a little service is held on the wharf in memory of Marcus and his crew. Colette stands silently as she hears Charlie and others pay their tributes to Marcus, and then she walks off silently, her heart broken. She takes a cab down to Pacific Avenue where she finds Lorf, sitting outside the entrance as usual on his ever-more decrepit chair. She picks up an old milk crate and sits down on it next to him. Lorf looks at her mournfully. "I knows 'ow youse is feelin'." he says. "I felt that way when my 'Aze went." Together, they sit in shared misery until Colette finally gets up and tells Lorf she's going to get a few things she needs from the apartment and then she would lock it up. Keep it safe." she says, "I haven't given up all hope. Marcus might still come back one day." And Lorf promises to keep an eye on the apartment.

By July, with still no sign of Marcus, Alistair commissions a promising young sculptor to make a statue of Marcus, which is erected in the little square near the beach where the first surf carnival had been held. A plaque on the statue reads:

IN MEMORY OF MARCUS 460, WHO SAVED
THE COLONY FROM EXTINCTION.

"And it should also say '**AND SAVED THE HUMAN RACE**,' says Charlie to the crowd when the statue is unveiled. "But Marcus was far too modest, and he wouldn't have allowed that."

Charlie took on the role of Chief Administrator and then becomes President after the new Constitution is ready. He has accepted the role humbly, admitting that he could do the job capably but without Marcus's far-seeing wisdom. "But I guess he has provided us with sufficient plans and inspiration for a long time," he says. "So now we just have to get on with things."

Julie makes an unorthodox First Lady. Indeed, due to her particular circumstances, it is decided to change the title of the person accompanying the President to "First Mate".

"I like that plan," Colette comments. "Then it will never matter what sex the President or the President's partner is. Julie's parties will be sensational."

Bronte House is repaired and opened as the official house of the Colony, and Colette, Karla and Julie start holding receptions for visiting country settlement heads and other people who have done good works for the Colony, just as Marcus had planned. Colette feels she will never fully recover from the loss of Marcus, but life has to go on.

"Part of me has gone, with him. My world will never be the same. But I must plough on, for the sake of the twins," she confides to Annie. "One thing I can do when I finish work for the day is work on my official *History of the Colony*, which I can update as time goes on."

Life drags on for Colette, month-after-month. The babies grow and she's thankful she has them. The next Christmas, Colette and Annie take the twins down to the yellow Gully House for Christmas lunch.

As she sits in a deckchair, watching Annie playing with the twins, who are now almost 18 months, she sees Rose, her little face animated, chatting away to Rory who has just toddled back from one of his regular inspections of the property, bringing with him some pebbles he has found, and a beetle he has picked up; *He'll probably grow up to be a trail- blazer like Marcus, and Rose is already showing her communication skills*, Colette thinks, looking up at the blue sky.

Oh, Marcus, **please** *come back,* she pleads. *You said 'history never repeats itself' ...does it?...*

25

HISTORY NEVER REPEATS

IT'S NOW 2097 and the Colony has grown and matured quite a lot under the guidance of Charlie, who follows Marcus's manifesto for change. Marcus has been gone now for over two years and Colette, still grieving, nevertheless has kept her ship in full sail, looking after Rory and Rose, now three years' old, while expanding her work in the Department of Communications & Culture, doing her weekly TV program, and acting, also, as Charlie's second-in-command.

On February 10, at the end of a hot and humid Monday, Colette finishes work in her office in the Pavilion and sets off down the path across the park on her way to visit the twins at the Kindergarten-Creche. A cool breeze is now blowing off the ocean, a sign that a southerly might make tomorrow a little less oppressively sultry. As she walks across the park, she spots a hunched figure, sitting on a bench, skewed sideways to hide his face. Stopping, she sees that it's Lorf, whom she hasn't seen for some months.

"Lorf!" Colette exclaims. "What are you doing here? Where did you get through the Wire?"

Lorf turns towards her: "Youse must come 'mediatly," he insists, "It's urgent!"

"What's urgent?" asks Colette. "I have to go and see the children. It's nearly time for their dinner."

"Na." says Lorf. "Youse gotta come now." And he stands up and tries to grasp her hand.

"OK," says Colette. "I'll come with you. But it had better be something really important."

They walk together up the road to the gate in the Wire and go through, using her pass, into Pacific Avenue. Seeing the apartment building up close again gives Colette a pang of remorse about losing Marcus. She rarely goes back to Pacific Avenue these days – only to check if the apartment is still safely locked – the memory of Marcus and their time together there is too overwhelming.

Reaching the entrance to the building, Lorf leads her in.

Through the gloom, Colette can see that nothing has changed. The same smouldering fire, the same foul stench. The same bundles of decrepit humanity sprawled out on dirty blankets around their languishing fire.

Then Lorf drags her over to one corner and points to one of the bundles of humanity clad in rags, lying comatose on a blanket. Puzzled, Colette peers closely at the man. He has a long black beard and tousled long black hair. *He's much younger than the rest of Lorf's group*, she thinks, still puzzled why Lorf wants her to look at the man. She notices he seems to be suffering a fever, his cheeks are flushed and he's shivering violently. Then he opens his eyes. Thy are hazel, flecked with gold, and Colette stops in her tracks. A shock runs through her.

It is Marcus!

"Of my god, Marcus!" she cries, scooping up his head in her hands. The hazel eyes close and the sick man falls into semi-consciousness again.

"Marcus!" Colette cries again. "My darling Marcus!"

Then she stops. *It can't be Marcus. This man with the black beard can't be Marcus. I must be having hallucinations. Marcus is dead.*

She looks again. Emaciated, very brown from the sun, obviously extremely ill – but it *is* Marcus.

"Of my darling, you're back!" she cries, placing her hand on his burning forehead. "You're back!"

She picks up her mobile and rings Annie. "Annie!" she almost chokes. "Marcus has come back! He's very, very ill. Come quickly to Pacific Avenue, bring your medical bag."

Annie is amazed. "Are you absolutely sure, Colette?" she asks. "You're not imagining things?"

"No, certainly not," says Colette firmly. "He's here, and he has a severe fever, he can't speak. Hurry!"

Annie arrives as fast as she can and is guided into the garage by Lorf.

HISTORY NEVER REPEATS

"Quick, Annie, Marcus is very, very ill," says Colette, still with her hand on his forehead.

Annie quickly and efficiently examines Marcus, checking his temperature (which is very high), opening his mouth to check his throat, listening to his lungs and turning him over gently to put her stethoscope into his back to check his lungs again.

"He sure is crook," Annie says finally. "In fact, he's in a very serious condition and we'll have to get him to the Infirmary as soon as possible. But first, I think we should try and get him up to the apartment, get him washed and give him some fluids – he's extremely dehydrated. I wonder what on earth has happened to him all this time?"

With the help of Lorf – who fashions a makeshift stretcher, once again using his sticks and clubs – and with the added assistance of a couple of the stronger old men, Colette and Annie manage to carry Marcus up the stairs and to the front door of the apartment. Fortunately, Colette still has her electronic opener, and they carry Marcus in and lower him onto the bed. Colette finds some towels and fills a basin with water, and they strip off the dirty rags covering Marcus's emaciated body and wash him. In one of his pockets, Colette finds a familiar little conch shell which she carefully removes and places on the dressing table. All this while, he hasn't woken from his comatose state. Annie covers him with a towel and gives him an injection of saline to start hydrating him. Then she injects him with something to counteract his fever. Finally, she takes some swabs to have tested at the Infirmary.

"We won't get the results till tomorrow morning, so I think it's probably best to keep him here until then," she decides. "I'll stay with you tonight to help keep an eye on him – but I'll need to go back home and pick up some night gear. Can you call me a cab?"

Colette, thankful that Annie is so capable, rings for a cab, adding that she, too, would need to go back to see the twins and to pick up some things from the terrace house. "I'll go later, after you return," she says.

As they wait for Annie's cab, sitting by Marcus, they marvel at his reappearance.

"He's back from the dead," remarks Annie. "But if we're not careful, he'll be back there again soon."

"I wonder what he's been through, all this time," speculates Colette. "It looks as if he must have walked the whole way back from the far north of Queensland!"

"It appears as if he has had at least malaria on the way, if not any number of other tropical diseases," says Annie. "The swabs I'm taking to the infirmary will tell us what he's got. I noted he has suffered a broken leg at some stage. It looks a bit crooked. That would have held him up for several months before he could walk far. He'll need some physio later.

"But I do need to warn you, Colette, that he may well not survive."

Annie's cab arrives, and she leaves, taking the swabs with her.

Colette remains sitting beside Marcus, occasionally saying something soothing to him. At one stage, he opens his eyes again and tries to speak. "Col..." he mutters, and then falls back into semi-consciousness.

"Yes, my darling Marcus, You're home. Just rest and know Annie is getting the best medical help for you. I love you."

Annie returns, bringing her night gear and a bag full of extra medicines, plus a stand to hold a container of saline solution, and, finding a vein in his arm, she quickly hooks up a drip.

Colette takes the cab back over to the Kindergarten-Creche and helps the Nanny give the twins their dinner. She doesn't think it's advisable to tell either the Nanny, or the twins, that Marcus has returned. It is probably best if nobody in the Colony is to know about Marcus's return until he recovers – if he recovers.

She then goes to the terrace house, packs an overnight bag, some food for dinner, and a pair of pyjamas and other clothes for Marcus, and returns to Pacific Avenue.

Lorf is waiting at the entrance. "'Ow is 'e?" he asks.

"Not too good at the moment, Lorf," Colette replies, "but we're keeping our fingers crossed. Thank you for coming to tell me he was here. He looks as if he's been through hell."

Lorf nods. "Just 'opin e'll come good," he says. "'e always wer a tough'un. 'Ere," he adds, offering a bunch of leaves to Colette. "I picked these 'ere leaves for 'im. They's good for 'eadaches."

Colette goes back to the apartment and make toast for herself and Annie. All the while, Marcus remains asleep, his temperature still raging despite everything Annie has tried.

The night passes, with Annie and Colette taking it in turns to sit by him. Hallway through the night, Colette lies down on a sofa in the living room and tries to come to grips with this amazing event. *Marcus is back*, she thinks, *my pleas to the Universe were heard! He's back. Oh please let him survive and recover fully!*

Annie returns to the Infirmary in the morning and later rings Colette. "The results of the swabs indicate he has definitely had Malaria, but he has also had Scrub Typhus – a very nasty bug caught from ticks that leads to extreme headaches and leaves the patient needing to learn how to walk again – and he's also had a couple of other rare tropical diseases. I checked the Internet and found that some new drugs had been trialled towards the end of The Best of Times. We need to try and get hold of those drugs now."

Colette is excited by this news. "But where could we get such drugs from?" she asks.

"We'll need to go out to a couple of the big drug companies that used to operate out in the Western Suburbs," Annie says. "They've been shut down all this time, but they still have a skeleton staff – not a tactful term, I confess! And we do have their inventories."

Colette then makes a decision:

"I think we should inform Charlie immediately. He's now the President, so he should be informed," she suggests.

"I'll ask him to get the Army to take you over to the drug companies and you can see if you can track down the drugs. I'll ring Charlie now while you check the inventories on my compudule."

Charlie is both surprised and glad to hear Marcus has returned. "My god!" he exclaims. "it's a real miracle!"

"I think we shouldn't let the news out till he recovers," says Colette. "It's early days and he's mighty sick. He mightn't pull through, though Annie's doing her best."

"Knowing he's back home with you will work wonders, too," says Charlie. "just call on me for anything you need. Of course, I'll resign from being President now he's back with us, and

I could become Prime Minister – nobody's taken up that role yet."

Colette returns to the bedroom and puts another cold towel on Marcus's forehead, whispering comforting words as she sits beside him. Occasionally he moans. She looks a him carefully. Under that beard, he is still the same Marcus, but his face looks weather-beaten and exhausted. *What has he been through*? she wonders.

Finally, Annie returns, with a triumphant smile. "I eventually found the very drugs I'd read about!" she says. "One of the drug companies' inventories was incorrect, or they'd run out during the Calamity. But the other company had plenty of stocks, so I brought enough for Marcus, and it's good to know there are more supplies for the future if we need them for other patients. Thank goodness the scientists in The Best of Times devised ways of preserving drugs."

Colette rings her office and tells them she's doing some research in the still-deserted CBD that day, and then she rings the Colony Kitchen and asks them to send enough food for lunch and dinner to 2 Pacific Avenue as she is working with someone on a project at that address. For the rest of the day, Marcus's condition remains unchanged. Annie has administered the drugs she has retrieved from the drug companies and advises Colette to try and do some work on her compudule to keep her mind off things. In desperation, Colette chops up some of the leaves Lorf had given her. "It surely can't do any harm," she thinks.as she mixes the chopped leaves in some water and gently puts some into Marcus's parched lips.

Finally, around 5pm, Marcus stirs and starts calling out, uttering words that are unintelligible to Colette and Annie.

"He's still delirious," Annie explains, "But it looks as if the drugs are starting to work on him."

"Or maybe Lorf's leaves helped," suggests Colette.

"Maybe, but probably it's the drugs," Annie smiles.

Marcus starts rearing up in the bed, his eyes wild, and Colette tries to restrain him, but he pushes her away and seems to be trying to grasp something above his head.

Annie helps Colette to hold him down so he won't fall off the bed.

"He's reaching a crisis point with his fever," Annie says. "If he can get through this stage, he'll probably survive."

Come on Marcus, Colette urges him mentally, *you'll make it. You're tough.*

Gradually, Marcus's fever begins to subside. He lies back on his pillow and sleeps, a calm expression on his face.

"We'll leave him to sleep for a bit while we have dinner," says Annie. "But I think there's hope now."

Relieved, Colette goes into the kitchen and prepares some more soup. The Colony kitchen has sent other food, too, but soup is all she feels like having at the moment. Annie suggests they keep some of the soup in case Marcus awakes and feels able to eat.

"But I'll keep him on the drip until tomorrow – it has glucose in it too."

As they sit at the dinner table, Colette turns to Annie.

"Annie," she begins, "I've never probed into your personal life, but do you have a boyfriend, a partner?"

"I did have a wonderful partner, a fellow doctor, a couple of years ago, but he died of peritonitis. Despite all the drugs we could administer, the bug was too powerful."

"Oh," replies Colette, "I'm so sorry. I know how you must have felt."

"Since then," Annie says, "I've had a few flings – not with doctors. But I haven't found anyone who interests me."

Colette looks thoughtful.

"I do know someone who might just be good for you," she says hesitantly. "I wouldn't want to meddle in your life, but there's someone I've been dealing with at the TV station – the director – who looks rather a lost soul. Would you like me to tee up an introduction some time?"

"OK," says Annie, "so long as it's very casual and he doesn't think you have a plan!"

That night, both Annie and Colette take it in turns to sit by Marcus as he continues to sleep peacefully. Then, as the sun emerges over the beach, and yet another clear, sunny day dawns, Marcus stirs and sits up.

"Hello, my darling Colette," he says. "I'm back at last. It has been a long journey."

171

Colette puts her arms around him and hugs him tight.

"Marcus, Marcus, thank god!" is all she can say.

Annie checks his temperature and pulse and declares he has come through the worst of his fever.

"I think it's probably best if he stays here rather than goes to the Infirmary," she says. "I'll pop in every day to check him, and Colette, you know how to give him his drugs and keep him hydrated. I suggest you tell your office you have a cold and you'll need to take a week off, as you don't want to spread it around the office."

From then on, Marcus steadily improves, but he's extremely weak and unable to walk more than a few steps when he gets out of bed. Nevertheless, his decisive manner soon begins to return a little, although he seems morose and brooding and his eyes are dull, haunted-looking.

"For crissake, Colette, please get this ghastly beard off me! And please could you cut my hair?" he demands, and Colette is glad not only to see his old personality coming alive, but also that he wants to get rid of his beard; she is thankful to see his old face emerge. She wonders when he will feel like making love again – not for a long time yet, she suspects – he is obviously still far too weak and traumatised and disorientated. She vows not to pressure him. *It will all be alright in time*, she thinks,

Gradually, sitting out on the balcony each evening with Colette, he begins to recount the saga of his journey from north Queensland back to the Colony – a journey of well over two-and-a-half thousand kilometres, because he had been forced to follow the coastline and navigate his way around swamps. A journey filled with great hardship and danger.

Colette listens, rapt, and sorts out and collects together Marcus's sometimes rambling recollections of his epic journey and puts them into her *History of the Colony* under this chapter heading…

26

MARCUS'S ODYSSEY

(This is a chapter from Colette's *History of the Colony,* telling the saga of Marcus's epic odyssey from North Queensland to the Colony, narrated by Marcus to Colette, sitting on their balcony each evening after his return).

"AFTER rescuing the stranded group of religious pilgrims up near the tip of Cape York in Northern Queensland," Marcus begins, "we were happily sailing back home when a severe cyclone came heading from the north towards us. We clung to the shoreline, and battened down the hatches, took down the mainsail, and *The Sophie* still bucketed along just using the jib, because the wind behind us was growing stronger by the hour. By nightfall, it was howling past us and we tried to find a suitable inlet to turn into, but the gale was blowing partly off the land as it swung in its circular cyclonic pattern.

I was at the helm and sent a command down below deck for everybody to don life jackets even though by this time most of them were asleep in their bunks, and our passengers were very ill.

The sea was rising fearfully, with massive waves as high as the mast. I was finding it more and more difficult to control the wheel. A thunderstorm then erupted above us, and lightning was crackling through the stays. It was almost impossible to see more than a few metres ahead.

Suddenly the mast snapped, and an enormous wave tossed the *Sophie* up like a leaf – made mainly of fibreglass, she was very light. A second wave then tossed us sideways, while a third crashed down onto the deck and we began to sink.

I shouted out to my crew member, George, on deck with me, to get down below deck to the passengers and the rest of the crew as fast as he could and get them out. I was glad to have George on deck with me – he had been one of the gang which had invaded

Pacific Avenue a few years ago, and he had turned into a good and extremely strong soldier-sailor.

"We're going to have to abandon ship," I shouted through the howling gale. "Get the lifeboat ready."

The *Sophie* was sinking fast and George was unable to get to the lifeboat before we went under. I found myself completely submerged for a minute or more and all I could think of was Colette and Rory and Rose. I honestly thought I was a gonner. Then my lifejacket popped me back to the surface, I looked around for George and spied him hanging on to a broken bit of the mast.

"They're all gone!" he shouted. "Can you get over to this piece of mast I'm hanging on to?"

I looked around and could see no sign of the *Sophie* or her passengers and crew. They had dropped to the bottom of the ocean like lumps of lead. It was just me and George left, desperately hanging on to a floating piece of mast, somewhere off the coast of Northern Queensland.

I shouted through the gale. "We'll just have to hang on to this piece of mast until dawn breaks and we can get an idea of where we are." It was a very long night.

When the sun rose, we were able to work out where the coastline would be, and we started swimming, still holding on to the piece of mast. I knew George was strong, and I myself was a strong swimmer too, so I felt that if we kept our heads and conserved our energy, we might manage to get back to land. We took it in turns to do the swimming and kept up a reasonable pace for about four hours. Then, thank god, we spied land in the distance. The two of us, heartened by this sight, decided to swim together, still holding the piece of mast, and we eventually reached land.

Hauling ourselves up a beach at long last, we lay on the sand, panting but triumphant.

"That was a close shave," George remarked.

After we had got our breaths, we stood up and walked across the beach to the jungle behind it. We then began searching for some fruit from the trees and found some juicy things that looked a bit like mangoes and devoured them. All this while I felt I was in a dream – or a nightmare – and I would wake up soon. We then went back to the beach and sat down and began to ponder our next move. The wind had dropped and we realised that either the cyclone had moved on, or we were in its eye. It turned out, thank goodness, that it had moved on down south and the calm it had left behind continued.

For the next couple of days, we stayed on the beach, eating the tropical fruit from the jungle, and recovering from the long swim. I was still dazed by it all.

We were just about to set off south along the coastline when a pair of Torres Strait Islanders emerged from the jungle, preparing to do some fishing. We approached them, and once they had got over their surprise, we explained our predicament, using sign language and gestures. They indicated to us that we must follow them, and they took us through the swamps and jungle behind the beach to a clearing where they and about 20 wives and children and about eight other men had set up camp. They indicated to us to sit under a shelter of dried palm leaves and they would bring us some food. It turned out they could speak some English – their forebears had been in contact with many Australians in the Cape York Peninsula, and had in turn taught our rescuers, their grandchildren, how to speak a little English. They seemed to be the sole survivors in that part of the land; the Ultimate Virus had reached their people too.

As we sat devouring one of the fish they'd caught and grilled, I asked: "Where exactly are we?" But they couldn't explain this to me in a way that I would understand, although they knew exactly where they were. I decided to accept their hospitality and stay with their encampment in the expectation that Charlie would send a rescue vessel equip ed with search drones to look for us.

I asked if there were any towns nearby and they shook their heads and laughed. "Not for a long, long way away," they said, pointing to the south. "You can stay here for a while, help us catch fish," they said, and we agreed that this was probably a sensible plan.

A few weeks passed by and George and I were now fit and ready to set off again. No rescue boat had come, so we decided to walk south along the coastline where any search vessel could spot us until we finally reached a town, although maybe the town would be deserted if everyone had died from the Ultimate Virus.

I had become friendly with the chief of the group – Rawa (or that's what it sounded like), though sometimes he called himself 'Billy', which, with its connotations of 'goat', didn't to my mind, suit his dignified demeanour) – and was helping with the fishing one day. I carried back my catch to give it to the women to cook, when one of them asked me to go into the jungle and find some fruit to go with the fish

I went into the gloomy jungle where everything was still wet from that morning's tropical downpour, and I spotted some fruit halfway up a tree. It looked easy enough to climb it, but halfway up, my feet slipped on the wet trunk and I crashed to the ground. The pain in my leg was excruciating and I began to fear I'd broken it. I tried to get up, but I simply couldn't. I shouted out as loud as I could and eventually Rawa and some of the men came and carried me into the camp where they prodded my leg and declared that indeed, it was broken.

They told me to wait and they would get a man from a nearby settlement to come. "He knows how to fix broken legs," Rawa told me.

As I lay there waiting for this miracle medicine man, I was suddenly overwhelmed with remorse and distress over what had happened with the loss of the *Sophie*. It was as if I'd been in a weird state of shock, since *Sophie* was lost in the cyclone and now the horror of it all was flooding over me. I felt sick in my stomach that I, the captain, had lost not only my ship but her crew and all her passengers. I will never fully recover from that tragedy. I also felt a great yearning for you, my darling Colette, and the babies.

I was overwhelmed, too, by the dire situation I was in; no means of communication, thousands of kilometres from home, with no compass, no money and only the slightest possibility of finding any kind of transport to get me back to the Colony. What was I to do? The only thing I knew was that I must get back to you, Colette, and to Rose and Rory, and to the Colony. That was the only thing I could do. But now I was writhing in pain with a probable broken leg. One of the women came to me with a wooden bowl of foul-smelling liquid. "Drink," she said, holding the bowl to my lips. I drank the liquid and began to drift off into sleep. Whatever it was it had numbed the pain.

Finally, the medicine man arrived and examined my leg. I was still very drowsy, but I recall he manipulated my bones and then wound vines around my leg and covered it with thick pieces of bark which he also tied with vines. "That's a splint," he said. "Now you must keep this splint on and not try to walk. I will come back in two days to see you."

He returned as promised and undid the binding on my leg and replaced it with a new splint made of dried banana leaves and thin sticks.

"Now you must try to walk a little each day," the medicine man said. "It will take many weeks to heal."

Indeed, it was over two months before I could walk comfortably, and another month before I felt my leg was strong enough to set off on the long march home, although I still limped. As I convalesced, I had many conversations with Rawa and began to learn their customs. They could be ferocious if they were attacked, but in the main, they were a peaceful people, enjoying their life on the beach and in the sea, going fishing in their canoes, singing and dancing on the sand, and making merry, enjoying the climate, which seemed to have only two seasons: wet and dry. The heat wasn't too bad although the humidity was tiring.

I began to wonder if I might be able to have one of their canoes for the first stage of my journey, and Rawa agreed to give me an old one they had hidden in the jungle. "Take care," he warned. "there are still other people here and there. People steal canoes. They are precious." I promised to take great care, and I also promised that one day I would come back to repay him for his hospitality. The medicine man came to see me before I set off, giving me some potions to take with me to stave off malaria.

I then checked with George about our plans to leave, when, to my surprise, he told me he had decided to remain with the tribe.

"I've never felt happier in my life than I have here," he said. "I've got a beautiful young lady friend here, and now she's going to have my baby. I'm sorry I can't go with you, but I've found my bit of paradise here."

So I set off in the canoe, alone, and managed to paddle a couple of hundred kilometres or so down the coast, calling in to little inlets from time-to-time to find fruit to eat, or to take some time to sleep. I would sometimes take out that beautiful little conch shell you gave me that long ago Christmas. Thank god I had tucked it into my pocket before I set off on the voyage. When I lifted the shell to my ear I thought I might be hearing the surf outside our balcony at Pacific Avenue. As I continued to paddle down the coastline, the sea was calm and azure-green, and I could see brightly-coloured fish swimming under the canoe. I thought I could travel for many days this way, but one day disaster struck. I'd pulled into a beautiful little beach for the night, and while I slept, some local natives stole my canoe, leaving me to have to set off for the rest of my journey on foot.

By now I had lost track of time. I had no idea how long I'd been traveling and vowed to a record of the days, marked on a piece of bark, using a sharp stone I'd found. I felt like one of those people in gaol I'd seen in movies, notching up his time on the wall of his cell.

At this stage, I was still hoping somebody from the Colony would come and rescue me. Every morning, I would make my vow before I set off: get back to Colette, Rory and Rose, get back to the Colony. I tried to walk at least 30 kilometres a day, but sometimes I could only do ten, having to wade through mud in mangrove swamps, or finding my leg unable to take the strain of walking any longer.

Weeks passed. My vegetarian diet was keeping me reasonably fit, and I was able to jot down not just the days but how far I thought I'd walked, to get some idea of my progress. But then I began to feel ill, very ill. From what the medicine man had told me, I was suffering from Malaria, despite having taken his preventative medicine. For about a month I huddled in a cave beside a beach, wrapped in banana leaves, shivering with fever. But I kept on taking the medicine man's Malaria potion and it seemed to finally cure me, or at least to fend off the worst symptoms, and I was able to continue on my journey.

By the time I'd managed to walk halfway down the coast of Queensland I finally came across some human habitation – a small beachside resort consisting of wooden holiday shacks and a few small buildings. There was nobody there. I came across a pub and broke in and decided to sleep there for a night or two. I also found a clothing shop which had sold hiking and beach gear during

MARCUS'S ODYSSEY

The Best of Times. I smashed the door in and took a pair of boots, some heavy socks, and a couple of tee-shirts, a blanket, and a hat to fend off the sun. I looked at myself in the mirror in the shop and got a shock – my beard was so long! and I looked like a vagrant, which, I suppose, I was. I searched around desperately for any sign of a bicycle or possibly a car, but there was nothing left in the little hamlet. I guess others had cleaned out anything worthwhile during the days of the Calamity, which had obviously penetrated even to these godforsaken parts. *Et in arcadia ego*, I recall saying to myself. (I learned that saying at school, back in the Colony.) The thought of the Colony and our beautiful apartment overlooking the beach, and my little yellow house in the Gully, and my life partner and my children kept me going. Would I ever see them again?

And so I trudged on, day-after-day. I got drastically ill again after being bitten by ticks when I'd been sitting down in a patch of long grass one morning. I began to suffer the most splitting headaches – the worst I'd ever had. Finally, I felt so weak I found a little rock cave near a beach and made a pillow out of dry grass and lay down under my blanket, with some more of those ubiquitous banana leaves to keep the sunlight out of my eyes because bright light made the headaches even worse. I must have lain there for a couple of days, unable to move. I finally managed to get up and found I simply couldn't put one leg in front of the other. It took me two days to learn to walk again.

One early evening a week or so later, I came to what looked like a largish town, a bit inland from the coast. It also appeared to be inhabited by living people! It was situated on the banks of a river with a bridge leading across it from where I stood. I started to run across the bridge, full of hope that salvation was at hand. *Civilisation!* I thought, *thank god.*

Then I heard a loud shout and saw a man wielding a rifle coming towards me. "Stop!" he shouted, "Or I'll shoot!" Of course, I stopped and put my hands up like I'd seen in the movies.

"Who do you think you are, coming into our town like this?" he demanded. I looked at him carefully. He was wearing some kind of uniform, with a silver star on his chest.

"I have been shipwrecked and I'm trying to get back to

my home down south – at Bondi," I stuttered.

"Tell that to the marines," replied the man, prodding me with his rifle. "You're just a common vagrant. Don't come one step closer, or you'll be dead and floating down the river."

I looked up and saw four other burly men had come along the bridge and were now standing behind him. They all carried rifles.

This must be a vigilante group, I surmised, *it's no wonder they're suspicious. I look like a vagrant, with my blanket rolled up like the old Aussie swagmen used for carrying their goods and chattels.*

I made one last attempt to explain. But to no avail – they grabbed hold of me and put their rifles into my back and sent me on my way. Shocked, I staggered on down the road. It sounded like an organised vigilante army had taken over the town. I decided I'd better not risk any further such confrontations until I reached what used to be New South Wales, where I knew I would be able to get help from some of the Colony's regional heads.

But first, I had to get past Surfers' Paradise, and as I gazed at its skyscrapers, I had fears it might prove to be a post-Calamity cauldron of crime and corruption. But no. When I finally got there, marvelling at the once-bustling resort city, I found not a single soul. I passed by strip clubs and gambling dens, all boarded up. No bright lights twinkled, no spruikers stood outside the clubs enticing visitors to enter. The whole town was deadly silent. I came to an empty 5-star hotel and smashed the thick plate glass entrance door and went in, crossing a marble floor and walking up a flight of stairs where I broke into a bedroom and lay down on its enormous bed – the first bed I'd lain in for many months. I fell asleep immediately but woke up later, feeling thirsty. I turned on the taps in the bathroom, but no water came out – I had been hoping to have a shower and get myself cleaned up. I remembered seeing a water cooler down the hall near the lift and went down and thankfully found it was still full. I managed to carry the whole damned thing back to my room and put it in the bathroom where I stripped down and had a wash from the water cooler after drinking several glasses of water.

I stayed the whole of the following day at Surfers, wandering around and looking at the shops. Wealth oozed from those shops; it must have been a honeypot for the carefree population in The Best of Times. I saw some shirts in the window in a clothing shop and broke in and took them, discarding my old shirt in a street bin. *How strange this is*, I thought, *Here I am, breaking into private property and stealing clothing, yet I still feel I should throw my old things into a bin to keep the place tidy. Nobody will come and empty that bin – maybe ever.*

Back at the hotel, its lone guest, I made my way to the kitchens, found a can opener, and raided their cans of food, enjoying some corned beef – the first protein I'd eaten for many, many months, as well as canned custard and fruit salad. Then I went back to my room, had another wash, and went blissfully to sleep.

Next morning, I went in search of an electric car. Maybe I might find one whose solar panels had continued to function? I broke into half a dozen before I came across a car which miraculously started up simply by pressing a button on its dashboard. *Eureka!* I thought, *I'll be back in the Colony in a day or so!*

I set off down the Pacific Highway, which was in fairly good condition, and began to relax. The car was performing well and the world look bright. I dreamed up visions of arriving home at Pacific Avenue next day, and surprising you, Colette, and holding you in my arms…

I saw the sign Tweed Heads and slowed down. Tweed Heads, formerly in New South Wales, on the border of Queensland, divided by its river, had been annexed by Queensland during the last stages of the Best of Times. Hence, we had never ventured to Tweed. For all I knew, there may well be people still alive there, but I wasn't going to take the risk of venturing into the town. Fortunately, I drove across its bridge safely, unhindered by any vigilantes. I was at last out of danger! Or so I thought at the time.

I travelled quite a way until I reached Byron Bay – a hippie retreat back in the last Olden Days and into The Best of Times. I wondered if anyone had survived the Ultimate Virus and the Calamity there and was delighted when a bearded young man walking along the highway thumbed a lift from me as we approached the town.

"Thanks, mate," he said. "We don't have many car owners around these parts. I'm Hugo," he added." He told me he belonged to a tiny community of about 30 people living on the outskirts of Byron in a cluster of old bungalows which had belonged to their grandparents.

"Their grandparents had all drifted in from the big cities during the Best of Times, wanting to lead a simpler life up here," he explained.

Noticing that my car was starting to falter, he leaned over and checked the gauge.

"You're nearly out of power," he said.
"Would you like to come back to our place and wait till your car's solar panels absorb enough sunlight to get you back on the road – from what you've told me, you've got a long trip ahead of you."

I accepted his invitation and we drove up a long driveway through a tunnel of lush trees and arrived at an old house with a large veranda at the front.

As we got out of the car I could hear glass wind chimes tinkling, and as we crossed the veranda to the front door, I saw a couple of girls lazing in cane chairs. Hugo introduced me and explained I was on my way south. They smiled vaguely at me but didn't seem interested in learning more about me. I noticed they were smoking something that had a slightly acrid smell. I'd heard about marijuana and assumed that must be what it was. Byron Bay's legendary hippie history had filtered into our legends about The Best of Times.

While my car absorbed sunlight into its panels, I joined Hugo and the girls for lunch where they shared a couple of joints with me. This made me sleepy and in a very good mood and I reclined on a sofa, listening to their conversation

Their sentences started off normally but tended to trail off, while my concentration drifted off too.

Towards 5pm I woke up, feeling alert once more. The marijuana had been very pleasant, but I realised my brain hadn't been functioning very clearly. Now I was ready to set off.

I thanked Hugo and promised to visit them again one day. *I wonder if they'll still be here by then?* I thought. *If those vigilantes were to find them, they'd be mincemeat.*

MARCUS'S ODYSSEY

My car was fully re-charged, and I set off, aiming to drive as far as possible that night, and get back to the Colony next day.

But my sanguine hopes were rudely, savagely, dashed when I arrived at Grafton when I heard a loud siren behind me, and, looking in the rear vision mirror, saw a police car roaring up. The driver of the car, wearing a T-shirt decorated with the exact same silver star I'd seen on the shirts of the vigilantes back in Queensland, gestured to me to stop. Which I did.

"Get out of that car!" the man ordered, as he stepped in front of the car I was driving.

"Put your hands up and lean over.' He then frisked me, and finding no weapons, pulled me upright and started quizzing me. He demanded to know my name and address and asked to see some proof of my identity. When I was unable to produce any proof of identity, the man bundled me into the police car and we drove off at speed. I tried to explain that I had been shipwrecked off the coast of Cape York and was now on my way back to my home at Bondi. I then said I wanted to see Reg444, the Regional Head based at Grafton – a town I'd visited on several trips. I recalled the beautiful mauve jacarandas there in spring.

"You'll be meeting Reg soon enough," says the man roughly. "He's in the cell next to yours at the station."

My cell? I was shocked. *I've been arrested by this brute who isn't even a real policeman – he's another member of the same vigilante group I'd run into before back in Queensland. What the hell's going on?*

I soon learned the worst when I was bundled out of the car and thrown into a cell at the station. I sat on a hard, wooden bench for several hours, calling out for help every now and then. A plate of truly disgusting food was shoved through my cell door, and I heard loud shouts and scuffling in the cell next door. When the gaol became quiet again, I called out "Reg! Are you there? It's Marcus 460 from the Colony. Can you hear me?"

In a low voice, Reg called back: "Marcus! I thought you were dead, drowned up north! Thank goodness you're alive, and here. I've been in this cell for the past three months. Thank god you've come to rescue me."

I replied in the same quiet tone he had been using, that to the contrary, I had been arrested too.

"Who are these people? I asked. "I had a confrontation with them recently, in Queensland."

Reg replied that they were members of a vigilante army which had taken over the entire area of southern Queensland and northern New South Wales. It had happened quite suddenly just over three months ago, although they had obviously been plotting and planning for some while before they took control. "We tried to send messages about this to the Colony, but these bastards intercepted them," he said.

I languished in my cell for several more days until one day another man, also wearing a silver star on his shirt, came in and started bashing me on the head, all the while bombarding me with bullying questions. Finally, he threw me on the floor and kicked me, leaving me lying there. I managed to get up, vowing I was going to escape, somehow. But, to my utter surprise, the chief vigilante came into my cell a few hours later and told me I could leave.

"Just get out of town and never come back. You don't come from round here and we need every spare cell for the locals who are playing up. You'll have to walk – we've impounded the car you stole," he said. "We don't welcome the likes of you round here. We've warned all the towns down as far as Port Macquarie to watch out for you. The bridges are all guarded by our men, so you'll have to find some other way of crossing the rivers – and there are lots of them." He then shoved me out of my cell into the corridor leading to the entrance to the gaol. "Reg!" I shouted, "We'll be back to rescue you!" And I stumbled out into the night and walked as fast as I could along the Highway until I found somewhere in the nearby scrub to spend the night.

The next week or so was hell. I found some plastic sheeting in a rubbish dump and wrapped my blanket, my precious conch shell, can opener and bark diary in it and then swam across one river after another. My clothes were drenched, but the hot summer sun soon dried them as I trudged on down the Highway through the Northern Rivers terrain. Then it started to rain. It came down in buckets and the torrents created an enormous flood. I had to shelter out of the floodwaters for a week before I could move on. Finally, I emerged from the Northern Rivers area and began what I fondly hoped were the last few days of my journey. By this time, my clothes were quite ragged and extremely dirty, caked with mud.

As I approached the old mining city of Newcastle, where one of our Regional Heads, Frank, operated a thriving little farming community, I planned to find him and get some transport for the rest of the journey. But I began to feel dreadfully ill. I had a fearful headache and a fever came on. I became so feverish I couldn't remember where I was or what I was supposed to be doing. I stumbled on in the hot sun, which wasn't helping me, and I passed by Newcastle in a total daze, collapsing on the roadside and falling into a kind of coma. I think it might have been a return bout of Malaria, but I didn't have any of the cure left. After the worst of the bout, I simply struggled on until I reached Sydney. I remember vaguely walking through the empty city, past the big columns of the old Library and then I recall walking through an empty tunnel and finally crawling under the Wire and coming down past the Junction and down to Pacific Avenue where I staggered in, and Lorf laid me out on my blanket and went to find you, my darling, darling Colette..."

27

THE SEASON OF LIGHT

WHEN MARCUS finishes recounting the details of his long odyssey from the tip of North Queensland to the Colony, Colette sits, stunned, and silent, as he leans back and looks out over the calm ocean, glimmering under a high moon.

"Marcus," Colette says finally, "You've been through a super-human experience! Your endurance and determination are mind-blowing." And she leans over and takes his hand. Marcus remains silent for a long moment, and then he puts his arm around her and smiles – the first time she's seen him smile since his return.

"Now that's off my chest," he says, "I'm ready to get on with things. I'm going to spend the whole of tomorrow thinking about what needs to be done next. Try and get off work early – it will be Friday – and I'll cook a special dinner and we can discuss what lies ahead of us. But now I need to sleep, going back over my journey has exhausted me."

Marcus falls into a deep sleep the moment he gets into bed. Colette looks at his peaceful expression tenderly. *He has certainly been through hell and back*, she thinks, *but he never gave up. The gods of the Universe meant him to survive.*

Next day Colette manages to finish work early and visits the twins before arriving at the apartment. She can smell delicious aromas wafting from the kitchen. Marcus is humming! He comes out of the kitchen and envelopes her in a big hug.

"Hello darling," he beams. "I'm back in the land of the cooking!"

Colette is amazed to see the change in him. Gone is the haunted expression in his eyes, gone is the listlessness. The man standing before her is the old Marcus. She's speechless with joy.

As they go out to the balcony Colette observes that Marcus had set the table there with a tablecloth and lighted candles in glass containers to prevent the wind blowing them out. In the centre of the table is the little conch shell Colette had found in Marcus's pocket when he had arrived back from his long journey.

"Here's to you, Colette," Marcus says, pouring her a glass of champagne. "And here's to us and the future," he adds, clinking glasses.

"This is absolutely lovely," says Colette. "Where did you get the candles?"

"I had to break our secret about my return," Marcus confesses. " I rang Karla and announced that I'd returned from the valley of death and needed some smoked salmon, caviar, a tablecloth, candles and other items of *haute cuisine*. Of course, she obliged and had them sent down to me. She wants us to come to dinner to celebrate my miraculous return as soon as the announcement of it is made public."

Over dinner, Marcus begins to outline his plans and explain his thoughts.

"My journey has taught me a lot," he says. "I had time to work out my priorities in life – starting with you and Rory and Rose. The Colony, too, is a very precious thing and must be nurtured and protected.

"My experiences with the Torres Strait Islanders made me realise that life is to be enjoyed because it is brief – indeed, my horrific experience of the shipwreck made me realise just how brief it can be. I learned a lot about the Islanders' way of life. They work hard, and they play hard, and their community has its own rules – different from ours, but sensible ones. On the other hand, the hippies I met later on didn't seem to be very well organised at all. I think their grip on reality is very fragile and I don't hold out much hope for their future survival.

"There are some serious matters up north with those evil vigilantes that must be sorted out quick smart. And I want, first of all, to get Reg444 out of that vigilante gaol! I'll get Charlie and his Army onto that immediately."

"Which brings me to the crux of what I've been thinking. This enormous country of ours needs to be pulled together as a nation – one country – fast. If we let it go on with separate little settlements each doing their own thing -- assuming there are such settlements, we're bound to run into vigilante trouble and other disasters. This doesn't mean that everyone has to conform to one way of thinking or behaving. Everyone in our new nation should have total freedom to believe what they like. We must have free speech and freedom of action – so long as it doesn't hurt anyone else or impinge on others' freedoms. But need to be united to face pressures from outside our borders.

Colette interrupts: "Marcus, you should be aware that the Colony now has a President and is a Republic. Charlie became President after you failed to return, but he says he's more than happy to relinquish the Presidency and hand it to you and take on the job of Prime Minister. Indeed, from what you're now saying, this would be an ideal setup because you, as President, can be rebuilding the nation while Charlie as PM can get on with the more day-to-day affairs of the Colony."

Marcus nods in agreement. "Quite so," he says.

"We must be prepared for the inevitable rise of other nations. The Chinese, for example, won't lie low for ever. They are a very smart people and they must have foreseen the Calamity and prepared for the worst by building deep underground bunkers where generations of them could live until the radiation passed. We need to be a strong nation ourselves to deal properly with the Chinese – and others – on an equal footing. Don't you agree?"

Colette nods. She does, indeed, agree with what he's saying.

"Yes," she replies. "So what is your plan of action?"

Marcus pours some white wine and continues: "First," he begins, "We need to visit all the old capital cities in the old states right around this continent, see what's going on there, contact any survivors, pull them all together into one nation.

"Heaven knows what we'll find when we get to other groups of survivors. They may well have established communities of a very different nature to ours. Just as long as they aren't destructive or a threat to us, they should be allowed to prosper, no matter what they believe and no matter how they organise their societies. Nevertheless, we need to pull together as one nation.

"We need to get a couple of small naval vessels, take them out of mothballs, fit them out and use them to sail around the country. No more fragile sailing boats! We need tough vessels not just to ensure a safe voyage, but also to signal our strength and authority.

THE SEASON OF LIGHT

"Will you come with me on these voyages, Colette? Your ability to communicate with people and to allay their fears, and to cleverly get difficult people on side, as you did with Alistair, would be invaluable. And I'd miss you dreadfully if you weren't with me. In fact, I simply couldn't go without you!"

"Of course, I'd love to come," Colette says. "And when Rory and Rose are a little older, they can come on some of the voyages too. It would teach them more about the world than any textbook. Melanie can look after the Department when I'm away, and Alistair can step in for me on the TV program."

Marcus gets up and goes into the kitchen to bring out a magnificent pavlova decorated with strawberries and blueberries.

"Thank god you're back, Marcus," sighs Colette. "I was getting mighty tired of the Canteen diet."

"I think it might be a good idea, if we design a new flag for our new nation," Marcus suggests. " How about you inspire Alistair to run a competition for best flag design? Some great graphic artist might be out there in the Colony, blushing unseen."

Colette thinks this an excellent plan. "But we should try to keep at least part of the old flag," she says. "After all, the old Australia did have a lot going for it. How about we insist that the new flag design incorporates the stars of the Southern Cross, like the old flag did?"

"Agreed," says Marcus, "and I suggest we see if everyone agrees to change the name of our country to 'Newstralia' – to emphasise it's a fresh start."

Colette leans forward: "We must make your return public on Monday, I suggest I send out a Media release on Monday morning and you make a TV appearance on the Tuesday. Then you need to be seen in public, going about your official duties, so everyone can see you're real and not some plastic robot. I guess we can keep the memorial statue of you down the beach and just change what the plaque on it says. Meanwhile, I'll get Rose and Rory prepared for the return of Daddy and we'll take them to the Gully House next weekend."

"Agreed again," says Marcus, "I'm dying to see Rose and Rory again – but they won't recognise me!"

"They're pretty smart kids," Colette says. "They remember all sorts of things from when they were very young. Anyway, the moment you see them, and they see you, there'll be hugs all round.".

"I'm so thankful to be back," Marcus says. "We have so much to do and a lot of big adventures ahead of us!"

Meanwhile, after they finish the pavlova, Marcus waltzes Colette into their bedroom, deftly removes his and her clothes, and, his eyes burning gold, he falls upon her like a tiger, and she responds like a tigress.

All is now well at 2 Pacific Avenue. It is the start of a new Season of Light.

OTHER BOOKS BY THIS AUTHOR

Titles marked with * are available as e-books and Print-on-Demand (POD) worldwide.

ONCE UPON A VASE (Macmillan Aust.)

BLOKES (Pan Books)

OTTOLINE: THE LIFE OF LADY OTTOLINE MORRELL (Chatto & Windus (UK); Coward McCann & Geoghegan (USA) *

POWER FOR THE PEOPLE (Svengali Press) *

GARSINGTON REVISITED (Svengali Press UK. USA, Aust) *

THOMASINE: Nerang and Gold Coast Pioneer (to be published 2020 by The Svengali Press) *